David's Star

David's Star

A Novel

Carol H. Bullard

iUniverse, Inc.

New York Lincoln Shanghai

David's Star

iUniverse books may be ordered through booksellers or by contacting:

iUniverse
2021 Pine Lake Road, Suite 100
Lincoln, NE 68512
www.iuniverse.com
1-800-Authors (1-800-288-4677)

Because of the dynamic nature of the Internet, any Web addresses or links contained in this book may have changed since publication and may no longer be valid.

Certain characters in this work are historical figures, and certain events portrayed did take place. However, this is a work of fiction. All of the other characters, names, and events as well as all places, incidents, organizations, and dialogue in this novel are either the products of the author's imagination or are used fictitiously.

Although it incorporates persons and events from the Bible, the spoken words and sequence of events are created by the writer. Where scripture verses are quoted or closely followed, the primary translation used is the Today's English Version (TEV) also known as <u>Good News Translation</u>.

ISBN: 978-0-595-47761-6

Printed in the United States of America

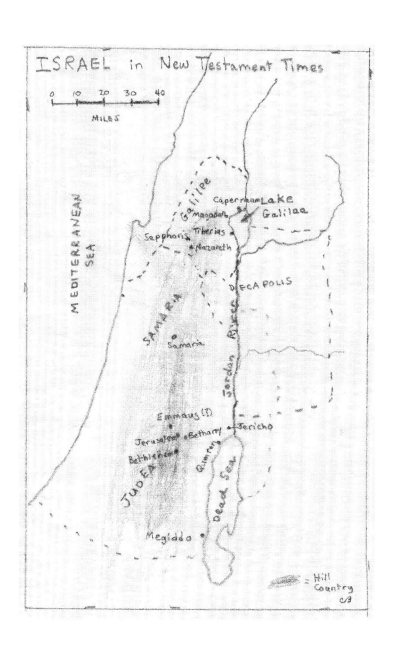

ISRAEL in New Testament Times

Preface

The Gospel of Luke tells us the story of the shepherds, the angel, and the visit to Jesus' birthplace, but when the shepherds return to their flocks, they disappear from the story. What became of them? We'll never know, but a fictional account, told from the viewpoint of the one of them might at least be interesting, and can provide an opportunity for readers to learn more about the political, geographical, cultural, and religious environment in which Jesus lived. This book is my attempt.

I am not a scholar, but I have taught adults in church for many years, I have one year of seminary education, and have visited Israel. And I have done quite a bit of research. The story itself is fiction, but I have tried to stay close to the historical setting.

It is my hope that readers may see the biblical story anew by viewing it through the eyes of a young shepherd who becomes a friend of Jesus, and a believer.

My husband Roger, who is a biblical scholar, has been a great help and encouragement.

I would probably never have finished the manuscript without the urging of my friends Lottie, Hank, and Betty who insisted I had a story worth telling.

1

Heavenly Visitors

It was my father's turn on night watch. The other shepherds were wrapped against the cold asleep under a tree about twenty yards away. It was an ordinary scene in the countryside except for the star, that strange bright star that had been in the sky over us for several weeks. I was sitting there talking with Dad, looking at it, wondering, as everyone did, if it were an omen. All of a sudden a brilliant light blazed out right over us. It lit up the ground all around us. It was terrifying! The glare was so intense that all of the other shepherds awoke, petrified with fear. Dad went to his knees with his forehead on the ground, while I, bold as any eighteen year old, just sat staring. There in the space between heaven and earth hovered a creature that appeared to be human. But he was larger than human, and all that light seemed to be coming from him. He began to speak, and then Dad and the other shepherds began to look too. I looked at *them* just to assure myself that I was not dreaming.

The creature's voice seemed to fill the sky as he announced loudly, "Don't be afraid! I am here with good news for you, which will bring great joy to all the people. This very day in David's town your Savior was born—Christ the Lord! And this is what will prove it to you: you will find a baby wrapped in cloths and lying in a manger." From childhood I had been taught that a Savior was coming. Everyone was eager for the Messiah to come and overthrow the Romans. However, I never expected the Savior to be a baby. I think all Jews held the consensus that the Messiah would be another great warrior such as Judas Maccabeus. As soon as the creature, obviously an angel, finished telling us about the child being born in David's city—Bethlehem, our town, the sky was suddenly filled with a large number of angels who were singing, their voices thundering in the night, "Glory to God in the highest heaven, and peace on earth to those with whom he is pleased." (Luke 2)

As we remained there gazing upwards at the vision, the sky suddenly returned to normal—except for the unusual star that still appeared to point directly at us.

We all totally forgot the sheep! After something like that, you can't be rational. We just gradually found our voices and determined to go immediately into town to find this miraculous baby. There were only two stables in town, the one at the inn, used generally by visitors, and the one owned by Micah, who bought and sold animals. Since anyone but a visitor would have given birth in her own home, we rushed to the inn. As we entered the stable we could hear the bleating of goats. The innkeeper's two cows were lowing loudly, almost drowning out the goats. The stable had several stalls for the innkeeper's milk animals and also for the burros of the guests. We could see the dim flickering of two oil lamps in the inner-most stall. Then, above the noise of the animals, we heard the high-pitched cry of an infant. We slowed our steps as we approached the lighted area. Here, amid the smells of dung and hay along with whiffs of the oil lamps' smoke, we found the newborn baby announced by the angels. The husband looked old enough to be the father of the amazingly beautiful young mother! I found myself staring in awe at the breathtaking dark haired girl holding the newborn tightly against her body. Her face was pale. This accentuated her dark eyes and dark arched eyebrows with long curling lashes fluttering up to look at six dusty shepherds and then back to her tiny treasure. I heard my father saying, "Sir, we are very sorry to be coming into your humble lodgings. I need to explain. We were caring for our sheep on the hillside there," with that Dad pointed in the direction from which we had come, "when the sky was suddenly lit up with a bright light. The light came from a man—well, he appeared to be a man, who was suspended in the sky above us. This angel announced to us that the savior had been born tonight. The angel instructed us to come and find this baby. He called your baby—this tiny child your wife holds—the Prince of Peace and the Savior. Surely you saw the light! It was brighter than the sun. And after this angel finished telling us to come here he was joined by a large number of angels who sang loudly. Did you hear them?"

The man spoke. "My name is Joseph and my wife is Mary. We have named our son Jesus." I immediately realized that this child had the Aramaic name for "savior" which in Hebrew is Joshua, my father's name. I had hardly taken my eyes off of the lovely girl. She looked up into my eyes, instantly averting hers downward to her baby. Had her husband noticed that I was staring at his wife? I forced myself to gaze at the scene. I didn't want to forget anything. There were two oil lamps carefully placed in areas cleared of hay. Their only bed would be hay, but it appeared to be fresh. Even the manger was filled with fresh hay and there were cloths laid across the manger for the little baby.

Joseph spoke again. I don't know if he had noticed me gazing around at their lodging or just wanted to explain the unusual place for a special baby's birth. "We came here from Nazareth. When we arrived at the inn I explained to the innkeeper that my wife was in labor. Because of the census, the rooms were all being shared by several people. The gentleman had a servant clean this stall for us and give us fresh hay for our bedding and for the baby. He was very kind and we were grateful for privacy. The innkeeper's wife assisted with the birth." He stopped talking but seemed to want to say more. We remained silent. I watched Joseph and when he was looking away I would steal another glance at the pale and lovely mother of the Savior. Joseph resumed, "We are grateful to you for coming tonight. Jesus has been a special child since his conception and Mary and I are trying to remember all of the wondrous events concerning our son. Your experience with the angels is very special indeed. We will never forget you."

Uncle Nathan spoke this time, "Sir, we are shepherds. We are worthless in the eyes of our Jewish leadership. Have you had other visitors?"

"No," said the father. "No, but you are not worthless in the eyes of God. He chose to send angels to you—not to Jewish leaders."

By this time the child had gone to sleep. I realized that the animals were now quiet. I heard a tiny bleat of a kid goat and then the sound of it suckling its mother. The burro in the adjacent stall was alert but this humble place had become calm and quiet. The shepherds who were fathers were gazing at the tiny red face of the baby. I looked at Joseph and looked longingly again at Mary before we took our departure. We left in a daze. The others were praising God and singing Psalms. I walked in silence; seeing in my mind a beautiful young dark eyed girl … so pure that God selected her to mother this savior announced by angels to lowly shepherds. I was already developing plans to see her again. Since the parents needed time to rest and recover from their trip to Bethlehem for the census, I was hoping that we could invite them to stay in our home, in the very room that I had built for my mother before I reached the age to follow my father as a shepherd.

When I reached sixteen years of age, I was still staying home with my mother. I had been born after several miscarriages and when my parents were older. They never had another child so I spent much time with my mother until I reached seventeen and began to learn about keeping sheep. My mother would card and spin the wool that we sheared from our flock. My father and his brother, Uncle Nathan, owned some seventy sheep and sheared them annually, giving the wool to my mother to convert into garments. In fact, for my seventeenth birthday, Mama had made for me a very fine cloak. It was the best she had ever woven. She used special dyes that we had purchased in Jerusalem and Jericho and she made it without seams, which required great skill. I was wearing this coat when we saw the baby. During my final year at home I had decided that Mama needed more space for her spinning and weaving. I talked with Amos, a builder in Bethlehem, and using techniques he taught me, added a room to our home so that Mama wouldn't have to put up all of her wool every time we came home. This was the room I determined to offer to the family from Nazareth until they were ready to travel again.

The next morning the shepherds took turns leaving the sheep to go home and tell their families about the amazing night. When Uncle Nathan returned, I asked Dad if I could be next. When I rushed into the house, breathless from running from the fields, I could hardly speak. "Mama," I gasped. "Mama, last night Dad and I were awake watching that star that has been hovering over Bethlehem for several weeks. Suddenly we saw a brilliant light and a man—an angel—was suspended between heaven and earth and telling us—shepherds—about the birth of the Savior! He also called him the Prince of Peace. Mama, why would God send angels to shepherds? The angel was joined by many other angels who sang loudly. Mama, did you hear singing last night? Did you see a bright light? It was all bright and loud!"

"No, David. I was very tired and perhaps sleeping too soundly. Why would God announce this to shepherds? Well, maybe God loves shepherds more than the priests do. Maybe God loves shepherds as much as I love two very special shepherds."

I rushed on to what had been lingering in my mind from the moment I turned my back on fabulous Mary. "Mama, these people are a long way from their home. They are from Nazareth. They had to come here for Herod's census. Mama, they are in a barn. Would it be all right for us to allow them to stay in our extra room until they are ready to travel again? It doesn't seem right for them to have to live in a stable. You would have to work in this part of the house but it would only be for a short while."

"David, of course these special people are welcome to come to our house. I will prepare the room for them. You return to the stable and bring them back right away. Even if this were not a special baby they would be welcome here. A newborn needs a cleaner home than a place with cattle and burros. When you get here I'll have the room ready."

Tears welled in my eyes. Of course my mother would welcome this special family. As I rushed out of the door I turned and shouted a thank you to my mother. Our house is in town so the trip to the inn was short. This time I called out from the entrance to the stable. Although I would have loved to see beautiful Mary nursing her little baby I knew that she might not want a strange boy her age invading her privacy. However, Joseph called out for me to come. "Joseph, sir, this morning I went home and talked with my mother. Our house has a room she uses for her weaving." Then I wondered if this man even remembered me from last night. "I was one of the shepherds here last night. My father was the one who told you about the angels. My name is David. My parents and I invite you to stay in our home until you are ready to travel again. We would be honored if you would come."

"David," spoke the father, "we are humble people but a house would certainly be a better place for my wife to recover her strength and for her to keep Jesus clean. If this is not an inconvenience we gratefully accept your generous offer."

"I can help you pack your burro. I will lead you to our home. My father and I are staying in the fields at night and so my mother will enjoy having your company." I helped Joseph carry their rather meager belongings so that Mary, carrying her precious infant, could ride the burro. I was filled with envy as Joseph gently lifted his slender wife onto the animal. He took the child from the manger and placed him in his mother's arms. Again I had to fight the urge to stare at her. There were no other distractions today and I would certainly be noticed if I looked upon her as I had last night. As we approached our house I saw my mother waiting in the doorway to the added room. She had chosen one of Aunt Ruth's baskets and lined it with the carded fleece of lambs for the baby's bed. Mama's nimble fingers weave rapidly and we had not traded her work recently for supplies. So there were several beautiful new woolen blankets on the floor for the parents to use for a bed. The baby awoke as Joseph took him from his mother and handed him to my mother in order to assist Mary in dismounting. He supported her as he led her to the pallet on the floor. My heart pounded in my ears as I watched Joseph gently lower the exhausted new mother to the bed. Jesus began crying loudly in spite of my mother's gentle care. Realizing that only Mary could respond to that cry I took my leave.

I went to some neighbors, telling them about the experience last night and that the family was staying with us for a while. The families of the shepherds believed me about the vision, but other families thought it was ridiculous that God would have the savior born in a barn and invite *shepherds* as the only witnesses of the event. The rabbi of our synagogue laughed at me and asked me what we were drinking last night. I had liked him until that time. He said he was awake studying last night and he never saw a bright light nor heard *angels*. "If God sends the Messiah, David, be assured that he will notify us before he sends word to *shepherds*." I was angry and humiliated as I returned to the flock. I did my duties with resentment in my heart, especially towards the rabbi who had ridiculed us. We were good enough for the angels but not for our rabbi.

That night I fell into a restless sleep, wrapped in my coat. I kept seeing that angel and hearing the chorus of angels praising God and promising peace. How could a baby bring peace? If this baby could get us out from under the iron hand of the Romans he would be welcome indeed. But that would mean many more years of oppression to allow the baby to become a man. I would wake up and my mind kept returning to Mary—beautiful Mary. Then I kept thinking how terrible I was to be obsessed with a married woman. I would drift back to sleep and again see the angels or the soft pale face with beautiful eyes.

During the next few days I went home twice. It was always a joy to see my mother, but I also treasured every minute that I spent with the family from Nazareth.

Mary turned her dark eyes on me and said gently, "Would you like to hold him?"

"I … I don't know how." I admitted. "I'm afraid I might hurt him." I added.

She didn't reply but took the tiny bundle and laid it in my arms. It seemed strange to be holding a tiny baby with knowledge that somehow this baby was the Savior; that this baby was going to bring peace to our troubled world. As I rocked my body and watched the infant, I convinced myself that he was smiling at me.

When I told Dad about it, he laughed. "You didn't smile at me when you were a week old. In fact, I think you cried every time I held you for two months."

I looked at my father and grinned, "I must do it better than you!"

After Joseph and his family had been at our house for ten days, Dad and I saw a strange caravan coming over the hill towards us as we tended our flock. There were two men riding on camels. That is a funny sight because the animals are so silly looking and seem to wobble so when they walk that it amazes me that anyone could ride the beasts, or for that matter, would want to. The men were dressed in clothes that shone in the sunlight, obviously not wool or homespun. One of the two men on camels had gold threads woven into his cloak. I knew these men were surely rich. In their entourage were four servants and several burros carrying their possessions. They approached Dad and me and one of them dismounted. He spoke Aramaic and asked a question that only we shepherds would understand fully. "We are looking for the baby who is to become the King of the Jews. We've been following his star and it leads us here." I was astonished. How did these foreigners learn about the birth of Jesus? I went with these men, leading them to my own house. As we walked over the hills towards Bethlehem I asked the man who had dismounted how they learned about this birth. "We are astrologers. We saw his star and our studies led us to seek the one who was to be born King of the Jews."

"King of the Jews?" I thought. "Here is yet another title for a tiny newborn infant." I was again amazed about the revelation of this birth. Obviously this child Jesus was everything the angels had said. Here were astrologers from the East who had been led from a great distance and over a long period of time by the unusual star. And they knew about the miracle child—even before he was born they had set out to find him. How could shepherds and astrologers from the east know about this fantastic event when the rabbi, priests and other religious leaders had not been told anything?

When we arrived at the house I stood back and watched the two men enter the room where Mary and baby Jesus were resting. I remained outside with their servants, watching through the doorway as these men presented to Mary their gifts for the child. One presented her with a beautiful golden pendant. The goldsmith had artfully inscribed the star with the tail. This was an awesome gift. The other man gave her two perfumes: frankincense and myrrh. Since these are oriental resins, I had never smelled them before. I was aware that they were rare and precious. These men bowed down and worshipped the dark haired infant. It was a strange sensation watching these people who had come so far and journeyed for such a long time worshipping a tiny newborn baby. After the men left, I asked if I could see the gifts. Mary opened the perfumes for me. They smelled so sweet that I wanted to comb them through her hair with my fingers or put them on her delicate wrists. Realizing that the family would be leaving soon I determined that I, too, must give a gift to the child. Having very few possessions, I thought long and hard about a gift for Jesus. When I realized what I must give him, I went to my mother, who had labored many hours creating a beautiful seamless coat for me. I prayed she would understand that this must be my gift for the child. I went to her and knelt beside her as she worked. "Mama, you saw those men give gifts to Jesus. I feel that I, too, must give a gift." I took a deep breath and paused. "I want to give the Savior my most treasured possession … Mama; I want to give him my coat. When he becomes a man, he will have the finest coat in all Judea." I think Mama realized what I was going to say even before I opened my mouth. Her smile as she nodded made the joy of presenting a gift to Jesus even more significant. And Mary's smile melted my heart. I blushed as she thanked me for such a personal gift, promising me that Jesus would wear that fine coat with honor and that she would always remember the hospitality of Joshua, Martha and David in sharing their home with strangers.

On the day that Mary and Joseph were to depart, I went home to see them off. Joseph told me that an angel had told him to go to Egypt rather than back to Nazareth. King Herod had learned about the birth of a child who was to become King of the Jews. In order to prevent someone from overthrowing his kingdom, he was planning to kill the baby. So, as Joseph, Mary and Jesus slowly faded from sight, I was praying that King Herod would not find them.

A week after their departure I had the most horrible experience in my entire life. Herod had learned about Jesus from the star gazers. When he realized that they had gone back without telling him where the child was, he decided to be sure and destroy this future king of the Jews. He sent Roman soldiers into Bethlehem to kill babies. Word spread quickly after the soldiers had killed two children on the outskirts of town. Mothers snatched their children and ran into the forest and the hills. Two went to the field with the shepherds. Huldah was not well and her child was only three months old. She took him to the roof of her house and neighbors covered them both with palm fronds. The soldiers entered her house and recognized the accoutrements of a baby. Two of the Romans angrily ran around the vicinity searching for the baby that they knew was there. Little Amos was unable to keep quiet with all of the shouting and hiding under scratchy palm fronds. As he began to cry, one soldier rushed to the roof and stripped off the covering of palms. Holding his sword in his right hand he grabbed for the infant with his left. Huldah leapt to her feet and began clawing at his face, screaming and crying in desperation. Witnesses told me that the soldier calmly ran his sword through Huldah's chest and without emotion bashed the infant's head on the ledge to the roof. He tossed tiny Amos on top of his mother, wiped Huldah's blood on the palm fronds, and strolled away.

When it was all over, seven children were dead, along with Huldah. One of Nathan's sons, Absalom, came to where we were with the sheep. He told us everything that had happened. I thought about what Joseph had said about Herod. If only we could have known what King Herod would do we could have hidden the children. Perhaps we should have suspected that he might do such a thing. He had hired people to murder his brothers, his wife and even several of his own sons so that they couldn't usurp his throne. When he was first appointed King of the Jews by Mark Antony, he brutally executed the forty-five of the seventy members of the Sanhedrin who had been against him. But I don't think anyone realized the depths of his depravity. No one could think he would kill babies and children indiscriminately. It was gruesome! I cried myself to sleep that night. I was asking God how His Messiah, the Prince of Peace, was going to help our people. I was thankful that Mary, Jesus and Joseph were safe, but I was also grappling with God over the tragedy that had come upon our little town as a result of Jesus being born there. My hatred of the Romans hardened and I realized that our Jewish leaders held their positions by flattering Herod and refusing to stand up to him. I hated them too. They were all just like my rabbi—so confident that they were God's special people that they looked upon everyone else with scorn and disdain. At dawn I awoke sweaty from restless dreams filled with anger and hatred. I wondered how we could wait for an infant to become a man and save us.

2

The Death of Herod

A year after the birth of the baby Jesus we learned of the death of Herod. In spite of the fact that Herod had initiated the rebuilding of the Temple and accomplished many successful and far-sighted building projects, the hatred in Bethlehem of the man was still very fresh on our minds. The grief from the murder of the babies was a permanent pain for all who lived through it. My father could remember when Herod became the king of Israel. Although the Romans appointed him to appease the Jewish population, real Jews knew Herod was a half breed. His only claim to the Jewish people had been his beautiful wife, Miriam. Dad told me that Herod married Miriam only because of the power with the Jewish nation he would get from such a marriage. Dad had seen Miriam and said she was very beautiful. During Herod's reign the rumors of his brutality were a constant reminder of how terrible the man was. He had several of his sons killed, also his wife Miriam, her mother, her brother and countless other people whenever he thought there was some sort of threat to his throne. How can a man kill his own children and a lovely wife?

The Temple project was one of the most impressive things being accomplished during his reign. He also established a city named Caesarea (for Augustus Caesar) which provided Judea with a port city, allowing shipping of goods to and from other countries via the Mediterranean Sea. Although he was building many pagan projects, fortresses and amphitheaters for himself and his soldiers, and several palaces for his life of luxury, it is commendable that he was rebuilding the great Temple in Jerusalem. It was being rebuilt on the very site of Solomon's Temple that had been destroyed by the Roman soldiers under Pompey more than fifty years earlier. The stories of Solomon's magnificent Temple indicated that Herod's Temple was even more beautiful and more luxurious than anything in those days of old. The aqueduct he had constructed bringing water into Jerusalem was a masterpiece. The great city was growing rapidly and water is precious in this arid land. Herod's aqueduct provided a permanent reliable source of water for Jerusalem.

There were always rumors about Herod and his brutality. Some of his servants told people we knew that Herod had ordered the murder of several hundred people at his death. The reason: to guarantee there would be tears shed at his funeral. Fortunately, sanity prevailed and this order was never carried out. Archelaus planned a magnificent funeral for his father. The casket was decorated with gold and this son went to the Temple to offer a sacrifice at his father's death. It was the season of Passover and Jerusalem was crowded with pilgrims for this most important day in the Jewish calendar. When Archelaus saw the crowds rejoicing at the death of his father Herod he became very angry and called for Roman troops. The angry crowds threw stones at the soldiers, killing some of them. Archelaus gave the orders to the army and some three thousand Jews were killed. So Herod's wish came true. There were tears shed at his death.

After his death, we hoped for a ruler who was sane and who cared about the people of Israel. Under the direction of Rome—following Herod's orders, his sons became heirs to his throne. Three of his sons that he had not killed were given the kingdom in pieces. Our area, Judea fell under the power of Herod's son Archelaus, Philip was given control of the gentile territory east of the Jordan River and Herod Antipas was put in charge of Galilee and its environs. So we Jews waited helplessly for a small child to become a man and save us from these hated Romans.

3

A Visit to Jericho and Qumran

As time passed, we shepherds wondered if anything was going to result from what transpired the night of the angels and Jesus' birth. Year after year I would keep track of how old Jesus would be and ask myself when he was going to be old enough to bring peace. When was he going to be old enough to save us? Ten years after the baby's birth, my father took me with him on a trip to Jericho. He needed to buy dyes for Mama, a supply of salt for curing mutton and several other items. The trip to Jericho was over the mountains and down towards the Dead Sea. In fact, I would get to see that body of water on this trip, as we needed to go up into the Essene community to trade some of our sheepskins for the salt and some oils for Mama and some other ladies of Bethlehem. Dad was getting old and needed a younger man to accompany him on this trip. I later wondered if the took me along, knowing that his health was failing and preparing me to be able to make this trip when he could no longer do it. The route led us through a small community just east of Jerusalem called Bethany. Farther along it would become more removed from towns and more dangerous. There were lions in these hills. But the greater danger was from the thieves that frequently hid, waiting to rob people going between Jericho and Jerusalem, as we were, to shop. Roman soldiers made a perfunctory gesture of guarding this road, but it was certainly always dangerous for travelers. Dad and I dressed in our most ragged shepherd clothing and carried our money under our loincloths. The sheepskins were supple and easily bundled. We made sure that any observer saw that we were carrying only sheepskins, which were of little use to robbers.

As we were passing through Bethany I noticed a young woman in a courtyard. She was very pretty, sitting on a swing, slowly drifting back and forth as she sang a Psalm. Her voice was gentle and sweet. Her sister came out to fuss at her for not helping with the chores. Although her sister was not as pretty as she was, she struck me because of her vivacity. She was pert, eager and glowing with health. Her dark eyes sparkled, probably in anger as she called out to Mary, her sister in

12

the swing, insisting that she come in and help with the chores. I felt sorry for her, but it was funny; Mary sitting there lazily singing and the sister trying to get something worthwhile out of her. After we got out of earshot I turned to my father. When our eyes met we both broke into laughter. "Well, son, which one do you find the most charming?" My reply was to simply laugh more heartily. However, I wondered if Dad saw the gleam in my eye when I looked on the delightful and hard-working sister. The sister was probably ten years younger than me and Mary appeared to be younger than the vivacious one. This lady lingered on my mind as we continued our journey through the barren hills leading down toward Jericho.

We were within an hour of Jericho when I saw the lion. Shepherding had taught me to always be watchful and my younger eyes were sharper than my father's. Because I had excellent skills with the slingshot, I always carried it with me. I stopped Dad, pointed at the brute, and stooped for an appropriate stone. The lion was perching on a ledge of rocks near the road only twenty or thirty yards ahead of us. When I rose from the ground with my rock, the lion slunk off in the opposite direction. I was relieved. Being a descendant of King David and named after him, I had determined to master hunting with a slingshot. Although I was very good, tackling a lion was always dangerous and I was glad the beast had fled. We completed our journey with much caution, looking behind, ahead, and above for some distance until we felt we were safe from the lion.

As we entered the outskirts of Jericho we were approached by a teen-aged boy, obviously blind, begging. He was probably about sixteen years old. He was slender and tanned. He was wearing clothing that he had outgrown and no shoes. We still had some of our food and could buy more in Jericho, so I called to him. "What is your name?" I asked him.

"Bartemaeus," he replied. "I am blind and hungry. Can you spare a bite to eat?" I asked him to wait while I unbundled my food and selected some cheese and bread along with some cured mutton. I placed it in his hands. His eyes were vacant and clouded over. When I asked him about his blindness he replied that he had been blind from birth. I thought how sad it must be to spend one's entire life and never see the sun, a baby, your mother, flowers … anything. Although I had seen blind beggars in Jerusalem, I had never come face to face with someone only a few years younger than me and blind. He seemed very helpless and fragile. He hungrily ate the food. I walked on with my father, looking back at the smiling boy eating the bread and cheese.

We walked a little out of our way in order to see the luxurious palace Herod the Great had built for himself south of Jericho on Wadi Qelt. There near the

Jordan River was a high walled compound with exotic flowers draping the walls and armed guards patrolling the grounds. The palace appeared to be large enough to house the entire population of Bethlehem. This terrible king, who had without conscience killed babies in Bethlehem, had fortified palaces in several places in our land. Jews were forced to pay high taxes so that Herod and his cronies could live in palaces wherever they wanted. Now his descendants were enjoying his extravagance that had put such a heavy burden on Jewish people during his long reign. There was a famous palace south of Jericho, actually in the middle of nowhere, on top of a mesa. Herod had named this fabulous construction project Masada. We were told how in that desert Herod had elaborate heated baths and all supplies to live in luxury for an extended time. He had gone there to hide from Queen Cleopatra of Egypt, fearing her anger at some of his antics in executing people who got in his way. We would not travel to this fortress. It was many hot miles south of where we were heading. Leaving Jericho, we traveled down the dusty road beside the Dead Sea, wending our way up into the hills to Qumran, a community of Essenes in a desert area overlooking the lifeless water. As we neared the compound we could still see evidence of the earthquake from about forty years earlier. Dad had spoken of the terrifying earthquake that occurred when he was a boy but in Bethlehem all evidence of the earthquake was gone. Rumors at the time of the earthquake were that this commune had been destroyed and that the Essenes had disbanded. However, they were quite organized when we arrived. This group of people was deeply religious, awaiting the Messiah, living apart from the general population as an act of piety. They spent much of their time copying by hand onto skins the Torah and the writings of the prophets. This obsession of theirs gave us a market for sheepskin, enabling us to make a trade for oils and salts they extracted from the saline lake below their community. Upon our arrival we were welcomed warmly and provided badly needed baths, good food, and wine. As they began to tell us of their search for the Messiah, Dad and I told them about what had happened in Bethlehem ten years earlier. We assured them that the Messiah had been born to a couple from Nazareth and would now be ten years old. There was an old man, the leader of the community, who questioned us at length about our experience that night ten years ago. We had been scoffed at so many times that we had ceased telling the story. Old Rabbi Bannus, who was almost blind, had memorized Isaiah's prophecies about the Messiah and was fascinated with our account of that winter night. It was good to be able to repeat the wonderful story without ridicule. Rabbi Bannus seemed to be in a trance as he recited some of Isaiah's words:

"A child is *born* to us! A son is *given* to us! And he will be our ruler. He will be called 'Wonderful Counselor, Mighty God, Eternal Father …'"

There was a long pause. We waited breathlessly. Then the old man said, "Prince of Peace."

The angels had said, "… and on earth peace …" (Isaiah 9)

Rabbi Bannus mumbled the next phrases and then carefully enunciated, "He will rule as King David's successor …" We continued to wait in silence as the Essene teacher thought. He called for one of the scribes to bring him the scroll with the prophecies of Hosea. He asked the young man to read a certain passage from Hosea. The words tumbled out, making sense to Dad and me—and to the teacher, "When Israel was a child, I loved him and called him out of Egypt as my son."

The old rabbi sent one of the men for the scroll of the prophet Micah. He spoke quietly to the disciple bringing the scroll. Then the young man read aloud: "The Lord says, "Bethlehem, you are one of the smallest towns in Judah, but out of you I will bring a ruler for Israel, whose family line goes back to the ancient times." (Micah 5)

Rabbi Bannus asked us for anything else we knew of that event. We admitted that we knew nothing more. The child would be only ten years of age. We shepherds never had occasion to travel to Nazareth. I had asked anyone who went to Nazareth, but no one had any information about a carpenter with a ten year old boy and the most beautiful woman in the world for a wife. The old man was bowed with years. His long beard and hair were clean and pure white. His eyes revealed their near blindness but his face radiated friendliness and warmth. We looked at that face aged by the desert and by years and saw a devout old man.

The Essenes were lavish with supplies in exchange for our sheepskins. Probably Rabbi Bannus had encouraged generosity because of our wonderful story. Before we left he made us promise that if we ever learned where the child was we would return to his community to tell him how to find the child. Neither he nor my father could realize how badly I wanted to find this child. I had never married. My encounter with Mary had left me disinclined to find another woman. It was ridiculous, but I could never let go of the mental picture of gentle Mary and I had not been attracted to other women. I did reflect, however, on the vivacious sister in Bethany. I was contemplating a way to make her acquaintance. It seemed stupid. I didn't even know if she was married, but I wanted to see her again. That aspiration eased my conscience of the guilt I held for my infatuation with Mary, the mother of the Prince of Peace.

4

Changes Following the Death of My Parents

Within months of our return from the trip to Jericho my father's health deteriorated. I watched him fade from a sinewy, handsome man of fifty-eight into a thin, weak person who could no longer go into the fields and who gradually lost his appetite. Mama and I knew he was going to die. I was needed in the fields to take Dad's place and yet I knew my parents needed me at home. I hired as a shepherd a fine young man who had grown up with me and I spent time with Mama and Dad. I was with him when he died. I realized that my mother was suffering deep grief at the loss of one of the two special men in her life. I could wait a while longer before leaving her to tend to sheep. Being an only child, I inherited Dad's half of the flock. With my inheritance and Matthew, the shepherd I had hired, covering for me with the flock, I decided to contrive a way to return to Bethany and find out more about dreamy Mary's sister. I cleaned up and put on my best clothes. Mama had made me a very nice coat to replace the one that I had given to the baby Jesus. I had actually asked her not to make it as nice as that cloak. Somehow it seemed wrong to own a coat superior to the one I had given to the holy child. I wondered if Mary still had the coat and if Jesus would ever wear it. I could still see the wonderful weaving and dyeing that my mother had lovingly performed to show her love for me and that I had given to show my love for the baby Jesus. No coat compared with that work of art from the loom of Martha, wife of Joshua. "Mama," I said, "When Dad and I went to Jericho and Qumran we saw a woman in Bethany." Mama began to laugh. I was glad to hear her laughing since she had suffered so much at the loss of Dad. "What is so funny?" I asked. My simple statement didn't seem funny.

Mother said, "David, when you and your father came back from that trip he told me that you had finally noticed a woman. He insisted that you were infatuated with a young lady in Bethany. Of course with his illness this memory slipped from my mind. Joshua was right. I asked him how he could think you were interested in someone you only heard speaking to her sister. Your father said that men just know things like that. He reminded me that the first time he saw me he knew he had seen the woman he wanted to marry."

Well, she was right. Or Dad was right. I wondered if Dad had also realized my infatuation with the married woman with whom we had shared our home. As I walked toward Bethany I tried to practice what to say. How can a man walk up to a woman and engage in conversation? This is not appropriate. Anyway, I made the trip and went to the street where they lived. The swing was still in the tree but neither woman was in sight. I managed to stroll by the house a number of times, but was never rewarded with a glimpse of Mary or her sister. I thought about asking a neighbor about them—it would be nice to know her name—but decided that might appear presumptuous. There was a young man there, probably a brother, since he was too young to be the husband of either of the sisters. He was working with tin; carefully hammering and cutting a candle lantern. I waved at him when he looked up from his work. Then I knew I had to return home because if he saw me come by repeatedly, he might wonder at my motives.

For the next few years I cared for the sheep, coming home frequently for short visits with my mother. I knew my uncle and his family were caring for my mother and spending time with her to alleviate the loneliness of widowhood. Mama was concerned that I was not making any effort at getting married. She yearned for grandchildren. When I realized that she was becoming frail, I began to stay home more. One day I had to go to Jerusalem to purchase medicine for Mama. Ruth was taking care of her much of the time and I could leave my mother with her sister-in-law. I decided to detour into Bethany and go by the house of the two charming ladies again. Of course, by now the whole family could easily be married and gone. However, this time I was rewarded! The sister was not only there, but her sister Mary was calling her by name. Her name was Martha—the same as my mother's. I prayed that was an omen. Since both of them were still in the courtyard, I assumed that they remained unmarried, though I couldn't imagine why, since both were lovely ladies. Anyway, I went to the well and managed to chat with some of Bethany's locals, learning that Martha, the oldest, Mary and their younger brother Lazarus, were all single. Still not knowing of any way to meet Martha, I reluctantly returned to Bethlehem with the medications I had bought.

I went and knelt beside my mother. She was lying in bed combing wool slowly as if she was very tired. "Mama," I began, "I learned more about the woman in

Bethany today. You will like her. She is beautiful and very industrious. And Mama, her name is my favorite woman's name. Her name is Martha!"

It was a joy to see my mother laugh again. "David, are you finally going to give your frail old mother grandchildren—now that I'm too old to entertain them?"

"You'll get better, Mama. My Martha will help care for you and you'll be teaching my daughters how to card and spin. They will weave a beautiful blanket for you to use after you get old."

We both knew I was lying but it made my mother happy. "I will have to confess that the Martha in Bethany doesn't yet know she'll bear your grandchildren. So you'll have to give me some time to progress to that step before I can bring my lady to meet you."

Again my mother laughed. Her calloused hands stopped combing the wool as she took my tanned right hand and held it in her pale, wrinkled hands. "David, any woman who knows you would never let you go. You go and tell young Martha that your old mother needs grandchildren."

I knelt and lifted her to hold her in my arms. The hard carders scratched my chest but I continued to hold Mama close to me. I didn't want her to see the tears seeping down my face. However, as they dropped to her neck I could no longer bravely support the lie. I gently lowered her back to her pallet.

Mama did not recover. She became feverish and died within a week. Here I was, a man forty-seven years old, unmarried and with no real family. This was a time of contemplation for me. If I sold some of the flock to Uncle Nathan, I would have adequate funds to travel. I realized that Jesus would now be old enough to be married and have children of his own. Surely he was nearing the age to fulfill the promise of the angels. So I took a portion of my inheritance and began my journey to find the Savior, Christ the Lord—as Isaiah had described him, "the Prince of Peace."

5

My Search

I made plans to travel to Galilee. The shortest route for this journey is through Samaria, but we pure blooded Jews would not travel into that city of half-breeds and therefore I would go through Bethany, down to Jericho and then follow the Jordan River to Tiberias on the shores of Galilee's lake. I decided to return to Qumran and talk with Rabbi Bannus and find out more about the prophecies. I knew there was a strong possibility he had died because he had been old when I went there with my father, but of course, to a twenty-eight year old everyone over forty seems old. I began preparations for my journey, which could last a long time and engender dangers I couldn't anticipate. I still kept my slingshot and practiced regularly just to maintain my skill with that weapon. I also carried my trusty shepherd's crook. This had been the downfall of numerous predators over the years and had on many occasions been used to retrieve a lamb that had wandered into the rocks and found itself unable to get out of crevices. My Bethlehem friends and kinfolk generously gave advice, a knapsack, food for my journey, and love. I had ceased attending synagogue after the rabbi had ridiculed me and the other shepherds on the night of the angels. Because of my hatred of our religious leaders I asked friends and family to avoid telling any of them where I was going so there was neither farewell nor blessing from the religious leaders of Bethlehem. I departed with a sense of elation in anticipation of my quest to find the young man Jesus and to see his beautiful mother again.

Soon after I departed I entered Bethany. Of course I carefully watched as I passed the home of Martha and her sister and brother. I saw Lazarus. He was tending a garden in the courtyard. Neither Mary nor Martha was around. Again I found myself wondering if Martha had married. She seemed to be about thirty years old. Mary was a few years younger and the brother Lazarus in his early twenties. I thought about this family as I followed the path to Jericho that my father and I had traveled years earlier. Fortunately, this time there were neither lions nor thieves.

Arriving safely in Jericho, I remembered the blind boy and decided to look for him. He was actually a total stranger but somehow he seemed to be a link to Jericho for me. Compared with Bethlehem, Jericho was a big city and barely knowing a blind boy was better than nothing. I found him very near the place where I first saw him; a man now. His sightless eyes were a distraction as I looked at his face. His clothing was tattered but he looked healthy, except for his eyes, of course. His eyes were forever clouded with the blindness but his body was slender and lithe, his hair clean and short and he trimmed his beard. I remembered his long name, Bartemaeus. When I called his name, to my surprise, after all these years, he replied, "Hello, shepherd from Bethlehem. What brings you to Jericho again?" His smile was warm and brightened his face more than bright eyes could have.

"How do you know me after all these years?" I asked in wonder.

"My ears are my eyes," he replied. "I don't forget voices; especially those of kind men. Your name is David. Is your father Joshua with you?"

"No, Bartemaeus, my father died shortly after our visit here. My mother died recently and I am alone now. I never married. Does anyone ever call you Bart? I have never heard this long name 'Bartemaeus.'"

Bartimaeus laughed so hard I began laughing with him. "I am called Bart by many people. In fact, since my parents died I am rarely called Bartemaeus. It is quite a name, isn't it? Tell me what you look like, shepherd," the blind man requested. "I have an imaginary picture of you in my mind and would like to 'see' you as you really are."

As we walked toward the well I tried to describe my physical appearance for a blind man: "I am tall," I began, "and shepherds have browned skin from spending a lifetime out of doors. My hair is a lighter color than most Jews. The sun bleaches it. In fact it is much like yours which is also bleached by the sun. I suppose I could say that I am strong because one must be strong to handle grown sheep for shearing and sometimes rescuing them when they go where they don't belong. Lambs are much easier to care for but sheep also need physical assistance and shepherds must be capable of giving them whatever assistance is needed. I shave my beard and wear my hair cut at the nape of my neck. Shepherding is a hot occupation and except during winter I keep my hair short." As I was speaking the thought flashed through my mind that describing coloration was inappropriate and I regretted using those words.

We reached the well and he invited me to sit while we talked. I had food for Bartemaeus. It was lunch time for me, so we visited. He knew a great deal about Jericho. "I learn much by keeping my ears open," said Bartemaeus. "It is amazing how much one can learn by just listening. Also, many people see a blind person and feel free to say anything, as if he were deaf, or stupid. I guess they think if I don't see them, I won't know who said what. I know almost every voice in Jericho, I suppose." He told me that his parents had died and he was on his own. He said some of the Romans would get him to carry loads for them and that probably because he was blind they usually paid well. Once they knew he was able bodied and willing, they asked for his help frequently.

I wanted to return to Qumran and visit with the Essenes, hoping that old Rabbi Bannus was still alive. I had brought a bundle of sheepskin for them to use in their copying of the scriptures. Bartimaeus had never been to Qumran and asked if he could accompany me. I was pleased to have his company. After a lifetime as a shepherd and having lost both parents, I welcomed a friend and the companionship that he would provide. The young man knew much about Jericho and about how to deal with the Romans. His advice would be useful for me in my travels. I stayed in Bartemaeus' home for the night and the next morning after having sheep cheese and mutton with bread and figs we began our trek into the hot wilderness to visit the Essenes.

We carried several skins of water and wine for the desert and the climb up into the hills where the sect continued to study and copy the scriptures in peace. They were obviously no threat to the Romans and had so few possessions that they seldom had visitors except traders wanting products they provided—primarily extracted from the chemicals found in the Dead Sea. As we began the climb up into the hills leading to their community, we met a returning group of shipbuilders who had been to Qumran to purchase tars for sealing their fishing boats. They were singing gustily as they approached us. When they saw two men approaching they suddenly sang much less loudly. The words were bawdy. I couldn't understand some of them, but their sudden change in singing indicated that they didn't want unknowns to hear the words, especially in the vicinity of this holy order. We greeted them genially and, recognizing that we were not of the holy order, their demeanor changed back to that of unrestricted gaiety. As their voices receded in the distance, I could see the walls of the copy rooms and several of the women bustling about carrying water from the spring to the baths and for drinking and cooking. As we entered the compound I had Bart release the crook he had been holding for guidance and led him by hand into the compound.

To my great disappointment, Rabbi Bannus had died. I was sorry that I was never able to tell him more about the Prince of Peace. I had learned nothing of Jesus since my previous visit to Qumran nineteen years earlier. I recognized some of the people there. And they, in turn, remembered me. They were glad to receive the supple hides I brought because they were working on the long scroll of the prophet Isaiah and needed more skins.

"David," the new leader Jacob said, "We've contemplated the experiences you and your father shared with us. As we copy we watch for references that could refer to the Jesus whose birth affected you. We have found a number of passages that seem to confirm this baby as the Messiah. How old is he now?"

"Twenty nine," I replied. "One reason I want to search for him is that he is now old enough to be fulfilling the promise of the angels."

Bartimaeus was listening intently. Of course I'd told him the story we'd told the Essenes years earlier. Bart knew what we were discussing. When the silence held for a few moments Bart queried, "Don't the prophets talk of the Messiah as someone who will give sight to the blind?"

Rabbi Jacob gently replied, "Yes, Bartimaeus, I was copying just this week passages in Isaiah that say the Messiah will bring sight to the blind."

Even though his eyes could not light up, Bart's smile changed his entire visage. Bart simply replied, "thank you."

As we visited, I told them of my parents' deaths and my journey in search of Jesus of Nazareth—now a grown man. The visit was, as before, exciting because I was such an honored guest—having been witness to the birth of the Prince of Peace. I was also able to tell them much about the Jewish attitudes in Jerusalem. The Pharisees and Sadducees vied for control of the people of Israel and the Temple seemed to have become a place for sacrifices without real meaning for either the giver or the priests who thrived on these donations to God. Because of Herod the Great's legacy, the leadership was actually controlled by Rome and the Chief Priest catered to the whims of Archelaus, Herod's son. The Pharisees were so obsessed with the letter of the law that human compassion wasn't practiced. The interpretations of the law had become so complicated that ordinary people couldn't possibly maintain obedience to all of them. I admitted that I hated them all—the scribes, Pharisees, Sadducees, rabbis, priests—all of those pompous Jews. The Essenes said this was one of the reasons for their isolation from other Jewish groups. They were convinced that the leaders were going in the wrong direction and so they wanted to spend their time studying the prophets and the law without interpretations by the Roman approved leaders of the Jews.

We were well fed and then offered "lodging" for the night. The Essenes were in a desolate area. Most of their rooms were reserved for copying scriptures. Their sleeping quarters were in caves nearby. We were taken to a rather large cave. There were several large clay jars in the cave storing manuscripts of holy scripture. Also, several of the Essene men slept there. It was much nicer than staying in the buildings because we could go back into the cave where the air was much cooler. Both Bartimaeus and I were very tired from the walk and the extended conversations with the leaders. I had been asked to retell the story of the night of the star to the entire group. I doubt I had ever forgotten one word or one event from that experience. I told them again about the magi from the east and about the killing of the babies of Bethlehem. They had studied the prophecies and again found more links that confirmed my story of that night. I slept soundly and awoke feeling exhilarated.

After refilling our waterskins and our wineskins, the Essenes saw us off with plenty of food and I again promised to return if I learned anything about Jesus of Nazareth.

Bartimaeus and I returned to Jericho. I wanted to move on down the Jordan River on my trip to Nazareth but Bart advised me to not start out at this time of day. He warned me of the dangerous areas and the wilderness where there would be little food. He said he hoped I found this Jesus and that if I did, please ask him to come to Jericho and heal Bartemaeus. When I set out the following morning, Bart walked with me as far as he knew the route. As I shouted my last farewell to him, I looked forward to seeing him again on my return.

It had rained during the night and I enjoyed the cooler earth and the fact that the dust was settled. I followed the Jordan River valley where I would have access to water and cool shade on the riverbank. The trip to the lake Kinneret [Sea of Galilee] was a three day trip with hard walking. My years of shepherding gave me good health and strength. However, I was not in a rush. The trip was an adventure for me, so I paced myself to walk one fourth of the distance each day. At the end of my first day I found a sheltered cave near the river and managed to find a beautiful area by the river and relaxed as I ate my mutton and cheese. I finished off my meal with dates I had purchased in Jericho. As it neared sundown on the second day, I heard a familiar sound—the bleating of a lamb. I followed the sound and found a week old lamb tangled in briars in a ravine. His mother was nearby. As I went to get the little fellow, the ewe became frantic but did not interfere. Of course these sheep did not know me and except for their predicament, they would have fled. I managed to get my shepherd's crook under the young one and gently eased him out of his imprisonment. After checking him for injuries, I released him to his mother. He quickly found dinner and was soon nursing, vigorously wagging his little tail as lambs do when feeding. Their fear of me gone, the pair had the new problem of finding their herd and shepherd. I sat on a rock and watched them, trying to figure out whether to leave them or stay and try to guard them from predators. The shepherd in me won out—I stayed. As darkness began to fall, I heard the sound of a shepherd calling—looking for his lost sheep. The ewe and her lamb heard and knew that voice. Before the shepherd arrived, I called out that his ewe and lamb were here, and following my voice, he came upon us. Grateful for my help and eager to hear news from Jerusalem, the shepherd, Daniel, invited me to join his group for the night. We walked together back to the camp. I saw a flock about the same size as ours sleeping peacefully near the riverbank. All of the shepherds were still up—two men and two boys in their teens. It was quite chilly when my shepherd friend Daniel took me to the group.

"My friend David here found my two lost sheep. David," he said, indicating each man and boy, "meet Judah Aaron, Michael, and Abraham." To these men he commented, "Thank you for waiting for my return. I've invited David to join us for the night. He's a shepherd from Bethlehem."

Since our occupation rarely involves travel—they were obviously curious. I explained my trip. "Almost thirty years ago a baby boy was born in Bethlehem. The parents were from Nazareth. They were guests in hour home for two weeks." Should I mention the angels? These are my kind of people but I didn't want to be humiliated again. Although my hesitance seemed to me like minutes, it was probably only a few moments. I made the decision. "My father and his brother owned our flock of sheep. An event happened one night while we were tending the sheep. I hesitate to share it with you because it sounds preposterous. Some people ridiculed me."

At this point, of course, there was no way I'd get out of telling my story. They might not believe me but I'd certainly stirred their curiosity. "Bethlehem shepherd, tell us your story." This came from the youngest boy—Michael.

"Well, one night my father and I were talking. The sheep and the other shepherds were asleep." As I related the story I was not interrupted. Looking from face to face in the flickering light from the campfire I realized their attention was almost hypnotic.

When I finished the oldest man spoke. "I remember the murdering of the children in Bethlehem. I was young and had a little brother and baby sister. My mother took us into the woods because she was afraid Herod was doing what the Egyptians had done and was killing all of the children."

While we ate they asked questions which I answered if I could. They were interested in the angels, Jerusalem, the Essenes, and the man Jesus. I promised I'd try to find them on my return trip from Nazareth whether I'd found Jesus or not. The warmth and soft crackling of the fire lulled me quickly into deep sleep. I dreamed of beautiful Mary. I'd not done that for a long time.

It was a treat to spend time with shepherds. They had a story of their own. They told me about a dynamic young man named John preaching north of here. I would travel for several hours before I reached where he was speaking.

6

The Voice in the Wilderness

The shepherds described the strange young man who had been preaching for a few weeks. His message was direct and simple. He preached repentance. They said he wore only the skins of animals and did not shave nor cut his hair. His diet consisted of what he could find or catch along the shores of the Jordan River, where he preached. They said his personality, his message and his delivery of the message were hypnotic. People were coming from all of the villages and isolated communities in the hills to hear this prophet. They were insistent that he was indeed a prophet. He attested to be only a voice in the wilderness proclaiming the coming of the true savior of the world. You can guess that my interest became intense at this suggestion. I am a shepherd. I have always been a shepherd. I had told them my story without ridicule. As I related the story, I had realized that this young man was now old enough to fit into the coat that Mother had made for me; every thread carded, dyed, spun and woven with love. I didn't doubt a word of their story of the wilderness man John.

My new friends replenished my food supply and gave me directions for the safest route to the Lake of Galilee. They also told where they had last heard that the prophet John the Baptizer was preaching.

I walked much more slowly than was my custom. I had so many things to think about. For one thing, I felt rather silly wandering through a strange country searching for a person I did not know, whose mother's face and voice had never for a day left my mind. I truly wanted to find the young prophet. Surely he was prophesying about Jesus, the baby of Bethlehem, the one who would bring peace, but I hadn't heard of this prophet or of his message.

This day's walk was uneventful. As I walked northward staying close to the Jordan River I saw the lush growth along the banks near the river but looking to the west I could see hills that were bleak with their barren soil supporting patches of growth amidst large areas of stones or soil heavy with clay. I saw some men on the other side of the river but they made no effort to call out to me, so I continued along the river, stopping to rest and bathe when I found an area which seemed safe. The gift of bread and cheese from the shepherds provided a good supper. I found a quiet glade of trees in a bend of the river and checked it carefully. Then I hid my valuables under a rock and spent the night in the cool grass beside the rushing water. I rose early and after only about two hours' travel, heard a commotion. I approached cautiously, waiting to determine if there were robbers or some other event. I saw a wild looking young man standing on a large boulder; his words booming forth with enthusiasm. I immediately realized that he must be John; the Voice in the Wilderness. The man's appearance was striking. His hair and beard were long. His clothing was skimpy—a loincloth of goatskin and a vest for his upper body. His shoes were skins tied to his feet with animal sinew. His deep voice was strong; ringing across the barren land and reaching his listeners as they sat quietly in the dust. I came within hearing distance and sat down on a rock to listen to the man speak. He was indeed spellbinding. The amazing thing was that John was not saying what people wanted to hear. He was calling his listeners sinners who needed to confess their sins and repent and be baptized. And yet the people were there—by the hundreds. They came in all manner of dress, some wore the clothing of the rich, but most were obviously peasants, and a number were dressed in the garb of the Jewish religious leaders with their phylacteries and tassels. I was surprised to see these people listening attentively to a man who was calling them all sinners. The way he talked was captivating. After about an hour, he called for those willing to repent their sins to come and be baptized in the Jordan River. I watched people from all walks of life come and walk into that chilly water with John and accept his baptism of repentance. He then announced that he would be preaching about ten miles north, again by the Jordan River, tomorrow, but today he needed time to rest and pray.

7

Tiberias

The following day I continued my journey in search of the young man Jesus and did not wait for John at his meeting place. I reached the Lake of Galilee and walked along its western shore until I reached the town of Tiberias. This modern city was unlike Jerusalem. Its buildings were built in the Roman style although there were many adobe homes scattered up the hillside which surely housed local Jewish citizens. The lake was beautiful. I walked out on a wharf to view the lake and the surrounding hills. I felt serenity as I stood near the still water after days of walking along beside a river that at times roared as it passed through narrows and had at no time been quiet. I was very hungry and was delighted to find a personable man cooking fish and bread near the boat dock. I bought fish and bread from him and he showed me Samuel's Inn where good wine was available. I chose to eat sitting on the rocks and chatting with the cook. He was enjoyable company. His name was Josiah. He had captivating red hair with matching beard and bushy, red eyebrows. His belly bespoke his cooking skills. When he laughed his belly jiggled and I found myself laughing comfortably with this cheerful man. He said I should plan to stay for lunch because he had been watching Zebedee and his sons and they had pulled in full nets several times. At noon, promised my new red-headed friend, Zebedee would bring fresh fish and delightful company. I rested there, watching the boat and waiting with Josiah for those fresh fish. I confess that hearing Josiah refer to 'delightful company' left me doubting that their company could be more pleasing than was his.

Sure enough, as noon approached, so did the ship, riding low in the water with its load of fish. Josiah immediately began to tease Zebedee about the quality of the fish, their age, their smell, too many bones. "These fish aren't even worth much as bait; not even other fish want them," the man joked. Zebedee warned Josiah that he would find another buyer who appreciated his skills and hard work. Bargains were made and obvious friendships manifested as Zebedee and his two sons James and John, both in their early twenties, began unloading the catch into Josiah's storage vat and packing them in salt. Each of the men selected several fish and requested them for their own dinner. I was introduced to Zebedee and his sons and given that same option. I chatted with the fishermen as Josiah cooked the fish. John appeared to be too young to shave. His skin was tanned and smooth. His light brown eyes were charming. He appeared boyish and handsome. James wore a beard, as did his father, but was also a very young man. In fact, his beard might be better described as fuzz. Zebedee looked older than his probable age, judging from the ages of his sons. As with shepherding, fishing is an occupation that weathers a person rapidly. Years in the sun and wind put false age lines on the face. Anna, Josiah's wife, brought out fresh baked bread. Zebedee collected a basket of fish and went to Samuel's Inn. He returned with several wineskins of a delicious wine which he generously shared with Josiah and me. James and John were quieter than their father but seemed to enjoy the camaraderie of the group. As we ate I watched these four Galileans, enjoying their accent and their obvious disregard for many of the obsessions of our Jewish leadership. I was strongly aware that I was not near Jerusalem. This was not openly done in Judea—at least not anywhere I had ever been. When the men found out that I had come from Bethlehem, they asked me for news from Judea and the areas I had passed through. They were especially interested in the young man, John, preaching in the wilderness near the Jordan River. Several weeks earlier James had gone to hear the prophet. He was convinced that the man was sent from God.

I asked the group about a young man from Nazareth named Jesus. He was the son of the carpenter Joseph. John had heard from one of his friends who worked on the Herodian building project at Sepphoris, a few miles north of Nazareth, that there was a carpenter, Joseph, with his son, Jesus working on the project. Word was that Jesus worked diligently and never complained about the overseers, the pay, mistakes that had to be corrected because of poor management. Jonah, John's friend, had told him that everyone wanted to have lunch break with Jesus because he always had interesting stories to tell.

I asked John the age of Jesus, but his friend had only said he was young. We enjoyed a relaxing lunch after which Josiah and Zebedee negotiated a price for the fish and the man and his two young sons returned to their ship for an afternoon of fishing.

I decided to stay at Samuel's Inn for the night and get off early in the morning for the hot and arduous walk into the mountains to Nazareth. Galilee was different from Judea in many ways. The people had an interesting accent and there seemed to be a more relaxed fellowship among the people than I felt in Bethlehem with neighbors. I ate supper at the inn and the conversations didn't center on "the law." Men seemed to enjoy telling jokes, laughing together and drinking enough wine to relax their tongues into a pleasant, though loud, chattiness. A few of the unmarried men were discussing the wenches they had enjoyed. The men at my table were interested in Jerusalem and Bethlehem. A number of them had traveled there for Passover but many had never been there and found our customs and attitudes toward Judaism interesting. They said they liked to hear me talk because of my accent. I was thinking the same about them. After our meal I walked back out to the now quiet lake and sat on the shore contemplating the journey I was taking and my many experiences since leaving home. Everyone I met had been friendly. I looked across the lake, seeing the reflection of the night's full moon stretching the width of the lake in a long line as it slowly climbed above the mountains in the east. I thought of the star with the tail that had pointed to Bethlehem many years ago. The words of the angels echoed in my mind, "To you is born, this night, in the city of Bethlehem, a savior who is Christ the Lord … and on earth peace, good will to men." We were not at war, but there was certainly no sense of peace among the oppressed Jewish citizenry. This area of Galilee seemed to live with less of a sense of subjugation than my province. Much of our repression came from the religious leaders rather than the Romans. I had stepped away from the religious establishment after my rabbi had made fun of us shepherds the night Jesus was born. However, I had been an avid student of the scriptures prior to that humiliation. I had no doubt that the son of Mary was the Messiah, but was trying to discover what the Messiah might do and when this young man might make his move. Then I wondered how he could free us from the Romans and be the Prince of Peace at the same time. After all, the Romans controlled the Jews with the sword, crucifixions, torture—an iron hand. Could a thirty year old Jew assemble an army of people to free us from the Romans and yet do it without war? There were clandestine groups of Jews who met and plotted to overthrow the Roman rule. The most active of these groups was the Zealots. I knew that when a Zealot was identified or even suspected, the Romans had him executed. Their favorite method of execution was crucifixion because the person was hanging there dying as an example to all who might consider opposing Rome. I continued to gaze across the lake as the moon rose higher in the sky and the bright reflection across the lake became first a light spreading across the water much as the star that had pointed to Bethlehem so long ago. Then the moon rose higher to become a glowing oval in the water.

To my surprise the sun was high in the sky when I awoke. The pallet in Samuel's Inn for which I had paid was unused. I was wrapped in my fine woolen cloak, the second that my mother had woven for me. Shepherd that I am; I had slept outdoors—contemplating the young prophet John, beautiful Mary and Joseph, the carpenter from Nazareth. And my imagination was flooded with questions about the young man Jesus. I lay awake for a while thinking about what I was doing. I felt rather foolish. Here I was, a man forty-six years of age, searching for a man I had only seen as when he was an infant a long time ago. I had no idea what he looked like, what he did or where he lived. I had made the assumption that he lived in Nazareth since that was the hometown of his father when they were staying in our house in Bethlehem. I hoped I could recognize lovely Mary with thirty years added to her age. I was certain that she was still beautiful and hoped I could look into those dark brown eyes of the mother of the baby announced by angels. As I lay there thinking, my imagination cluttered my mind with scenarios. In these successive scenarios I progressed from appearing silly to appearing a total idiot. What would I say if I saw Mary, the mother of Jesus, or Joseph, his father? How would I explain this quest of mine? I decided to stop thinking about it. I had come this far and needed to complete my journey. I had no doubt that Jesus was the Messiah. Surely the family would accept my need to understand what had happened in Bethlehem so long ago. Finally, closing my mental arguments, I got up and prepared to complete my quest. I ate bread and cheese that I had in my knapsack. Before leaving I wanted to bid farewell to Josiah and purchase some dried fish and refill my water and wine skins.

I returned to the inn and washed up; receiving jovial greetings from some of the men with whom I'd eaten the night before. They wished me well as we went our separate ways. I went to Josiah's fish market. "Josiah!" I called out.

"Hey there David!" he bellowed. "I knew you couldn't resist either me or my fish!"

"Well, you're right! By then I was close enough we could stop shouting. "I want to buy some fish and bread for now and for later."

Although I'd not said anything humorous, the great belly jiggled as my red haired friend responded—still speaking as if I were fifty feet away. "Young man," he said, although I was probably fifteen years older than him, "I can't take your money. Promise me you'll stop here on your return trip and tell me if you've found the Messiah." He was wrapping cooked fish and bread in dried leaves as he spoke. He then sat down and joined me in a meal.

"Actually, I'd have stopped just to visit with you again and to enjoy your food. You don't have to bribe me to do that."

I set out for the trek into the mountains of Galilee. Josiah had assured me that though there were occasional bandits, this province was much less dangerous than the mountains from Jericho to Jerusalem. Jewish pilgrims carry valuables to

Jerusalem and those traveling from Jerusalem to Jericho carry money on shopping trips. I, of course, carried my slingshot and my shepherd's crook; both of which I could use quite effectively in attack or defense from both humans and wild animals.

8

Nazareth

I was anxious to see Jesus and, of course, Mary. However I didn't move with haste as I wended my way into the hills of Galilee. I was seventeen the night Jesus was born. Now I was a man almost forty-six years old. I had already waited a very long time. I didn't feel a sense of urgency; especially since I had heard nothing of Jesus of Nazareth; this peacemaker announced by angels. Besides, the people of Galilee were different from us Judeans. They didn't seem to have the sense of total obligation to the Laws of Moses and the great rabbis' interpretations of these laws. It was pleasant to be associated with Galileans and to walk through an area that was not considered dangerous due to thieves. Herod Antipas was a tyrant but not in the category of his father. And our Tetrarch, Archelaus, was controlled in many ways by the Jewish leaders whom he in turn controlled because of his authority to execute whomever he chose. The Roman taxes were omnipresent, but most of the people of Jerusalem and its environs weren't really terrified of Archealus. And Jews realized that they were fortunate that Rome acknowledged our beliefs to the extent that in deference to our religion they did not require military service of Jews. I have always suspected that Rome also realized that Jewish fighters are tenacious and preferred not to officially arm a hostile people who could fight like our ancestors the Maccabeans and others had fought throughout our history.

So I walked into the Galilean hills slowly, contemplating what I would do when I reached Nazareth. I had come a long way to see Mary and her miraculous child. Would Joseph be alive? He was quite a bit older than Mary. Would Mary remember me? Did she realize during her time in Bethlehem how I looked upon her? Would I feel that flame again? The more I thought about such things, the more slowly I walked. I was formulating scenarios in my mind and many of them were unnerving. Although I rarely prayed because I did not attend synagogue, I found myself mentally asking the Lord for guidance. My obsession with Mary had truly taken second place to my curiosity about the baby who was to be King of the Jews. And, in spite of the fact that I didn't pray, I had become quite interested in the scriptures and researched those related to the Messiah. Our contacts with the Essenes had given me opportunity to access scrolls and I had copied several passages from prophets which appeared to refer to the Messiah and those which referred to the Prince of Peace. In our conversations with Rabbi Bannus, my father and I had, under the guidance of this good rabbi, found prophecies of a person who could be Jesus. We were especially impressed with the prophet Isaiah's references to the "birth" of a son. However, the question of his kingship still haunted me because in all these years I had heard nothing of him. Once, when my father and I went to the Temple, there were rumors that some of the rabbis had encountered a fascinating boy who was knowledgeable of the scriptures far beyond his years. This was during Passover and this boy had actually "taught" the rabbis. His name was Jesus and his age was appropriate for the child of Mary and Joseph. However, Jesus was a common enough name and there were no further reports after that time.

As I neared Nazareth, my palms were sweaty and my resolve was certainly lessened. I entered the town and first went to the well which is a common place of assembly. This well was a spring near the entrance to a cool and restful cave. Perhaps I could converse with someone there as I sought to refill my water skin. There were several women at the well. It is not appropriate for men to approach strange women. However, Galilee seemed so much more lax about the laws of propriety that I became emboldened enough to ask no one in particular if anyone knew Mary and Joseph the carpenter who had a son named Jesus. One of the women began refilling my waterskin and assured me that Mary and her children still lived in Nazareth but that Joseph had recently died. Jesus, the eldest son, was now head of the household. She directed me to the house where the family lived but told me that three of the sons were in Sepphoris as carpenters in Antipas' new city being created about four miles from Nazareth. I inquired about an inn and was directed to Nazareth's only hostelry, owned by a man named James. My food supply was low and my wineskin was nearly empty, so I first went to James' place and arranged for sleeping quarters, ate, and renewed my supplies. James was a chatty sort. It would be accurate to say he was a gossip. Perhaps this befits an innkeeper. From James I learned, with very little questioning on my part, a bit about the family of Joseph the carpenter. His oldest son, Jesus, was helping his mother provide for the other children still in the home, as were two other married sons. Mary was a beautiful woman who seemed almost obsessed with her eldest son. Whenever Jesus was in the village people would gather around him—even children sat quietly, attentive to his every word. The citizens of Nazareth took pride in the fact that people came from neighboring villages to hear him. Many of his stories were enigmatic but the listener was always fascinated and left with much to think about. Jesus was not married, but the other children over eighteen were all married. Two teenaged daughters still lived with their mother. Mary had not remarried after the death of Joseph a couple of years earlier. He had suffered a fall while working on a roof and not recovered from his injuries.

I managed to get away from the loquacious innkeeper when another customer arrived. I needed some time to think and to plan. I walked slowly through the town. I found the home of Mary and her family. I didn't attempt to visit because I needed to be sure the men of the home were there before paying a visit. The people of the town were surprisingly friendly. I was obviously a shepherd—carrying a shepherd's crook in case there was any doubt, hardly an aristocratic occupation, but no one appeared to look down on me because of my dress. Again, this was not like Bethlehem, a village in the shadows of Jerusalem.

I determined that I should wait another day and in the morning travel to Sepphoris with the workers and perhaps find out about the young man Jesus. My reasoning appeared logical, but in reality I had cold feet about approaching Mary and determined to approach Jesus or one of his brothers first. When I saw my bed at James' inn, I decided to sleep elsewhere. The straw appeared to be infested and there were several other men in the room. The shepherd in me took me out into the outskirts of town where I found a much nicer place to sleep in the open. I would save money and sleep in much better surroundings for the rest of my visit to Nazareth.

I awoke early and returned the James' for food for my day. I then found the road to Sepphoris and when a group of men began their trek to the construction site, I joined them and found them easy to talk to. When we reached the huge site where a number of structures were being created I wandered around, amazed at the enormity of the project and the lavish expenditure to create this Roman city in a Jewish land. I was careful to stay out of the way of the workers and especially the supervisors. After about thirty minutes of wandering around I noticed something that immediately caught my eye—and my heart! I saw my mother's cloak and knew I had found Jesus. Seeing the coat brought tears to my eyes as I thought of my mother's fingers carefully weaving a seamless coat for her only child. My eyes were blurred by tears but I had a complete mental image of beautiful Mary and her little baby boy. Here was that boy—a strong young man working conscientiously on a doorframe. He had the very dark and lively eyes of his mother. His hair too was reminiscent of the beautiful girl in the barn in Bethlehem. It was thick, wavy and very dark, accentuating the sheen of health and cleanliness as it glistened in the bright sunshine. He was my height and his slender body had the sinewy appearance of a person who labored. His beard was carefully trimmed and his hair was short. As he turned, my gaze was drawn to his long eyelashes surrounding dark, friendly eyes. He was a handsome man who could easily turn the eyes of any young lady. I watched him with fascination as he worked. His face was kind and his demeanor with those working with him manifested patience and humor. Apparently he was telling jokes, because those working with him would laugh now and then. I could not get close enough to hear the conversations. This annoyed me. I wanted to find an opportunity to meet Jesus and talk with him. My patience was rewarded. After I had watched for about an hour, the men took a break and those working with Jesus along with several others gathered around the young man in Martha's fine coat. Two Roman children edged into the group, eager to hear this man Jesus who was obviously the group leader. My long legs enabled me to walk through the seated group and sit close to the handsome raconteur. The audience encouraged him to talk and listened wordlessly as he talked. He was a good storyteller. His gaze settled on me and he said, "I see we have a visitor among us. Please introduce yourself. You are welcome here. However, be careful of the overseers. They don't approve of outsiders causing us to malinger—even if it is only in their imaginations."

I spoke slowly. I was not a Galilean; I was not a builder; I was not familiar with anyone there. "My name is David, son of Joshua, of Bethlehem. My parents have both died. I am a shepherd. I must be honest with you, sir. I came seeking you. You are Jesus, son of Joseph and Mary, aren't you?"

The answer was given with a warm smile, "Yes, I am the man you seek. Pray tell, why are you looking for me?" His eyes seemed to say, "I already know the answer."

I said, "I am from Bethlehem. Twenty nine years ago, when I was eighteen years old, I met your parents. I suppose I could say I met you."

He smiled warmly. "My parents stayed at your house, didn't they? And this cloak I am wearing was a gift from you—made by your mother. I am honored to meet you and grateful for the opportunity to thank you in person for this fine gift. We have to return to work now. Would you honor my family by joining us for supper and for the night? We live in Nazareth. When you get into town just ask for the home of Mary, widow of Joseph the carpenter." He walked with me and spoke into my ear, "My brothers and sisters have not been told about the angels and the unusual events surrounding my birth. My mother and I consider it best not to share this with them at this time." I assured him that I would not reveal this confidence.

I immediately accepted the invitation. The cold feet came after it was too late to back out. I responded to a very nice young man. When I realized I would be eating in the home of this man who was called the savior, I was overwhelmed. Being in the presence of an infant you know to be the Messiah isn't difficult. I was sharing the home of a person chosen and announced by God. This was awesome and frightening. I spent the rest of the day reliving those encounters in Bethlehem so long in the past and anticipating this intimate encounter with trepidation. I had expected to be obsessed with Mary—especially realizing she was a widow. However, after meeting Jesus, my imagination returned again and again to that smiling face. I thought about his anecdotes. They were not just rambling stories. Each had a moral and the more I reconsidered them the more I realized that this Jesus managed to "preach" through his stories. I'd never heard a rabbi with such an approach to teaching life's lessons. This Jesus would make a good rabbi. However, if rabbis in Galilee were like those in Bethlehem, he would never be accepted by other rabbis.

So, when the group of workers began the trek back to their villages, I wended my way back towards Nazareth. I could not find Jesus. There was a rather large group a bit behind me which I assumed was clustered around Jesus. He seemed to attract workers with his conversations and stories.

Since I already had scouted out his home, I walked directly to the house, arriving simultaneously with one of Jesus' brothers. He introduced himself to me. His name was James and he was the second oldest child. He already knew who I was and that I would be a guest in his mother's home. James took me into the house and called his mother to come and meet me. As she entered the room I felt my face flush and was grateful for the low lighting in the room. Mary was as beautiful as she had been at sixteen years of age. Her complexion was rosy, her smile warm and her manner gracious. Her dark silky hair still fell softly over her shoulders with only a few strands of gray visible. Her deep brown eyes sparkled as they had when she looked down at the special baby who lay in her arms in a stable in Bethlehem. The face that had been so pale on that young girl after giving birth to a child was now rosy, perhaps blushing. James introduced me as David of Bethlehem, a friend of Jesus. Mary replied in almost a whisper, "I know you. David, I could never forget you or your kind parents. How are your parents?"

I spoke very softly, assuring that only Mary could hear my answer. "My father died nineteen years ago and my mother died just five months ago. I confess that I came to Nazareth because of the experience when the angels came to us shepherds to announce the birth of the Prince of Peace. The vision of the angels was so real that I know your son was announced by God to shepherds and astrologers from a foreign country," I ventured. "I have never forgotten anything that happened that night and during your stay in our home. I don't understand it, but I remember it and I believe it."

"No, that was an experience that would be unforgettable," the beautiful woman replied. "I think I remember everything about that time also. Your father told us about the angels. I can to this day recite what he said word for word. I remember your sacrificial gift to Jesus and he is honored to wear it."

"I went to Sepphoris today and that was how I recognized Jesus," I confessed. "That coat was made by my mother and is her best piece."

At this point the man wearing the coat entered the house along with another brother. Introductions were given to all family members. Mary introduced me as the shepherd who shared his home with them after Jesus was born and the person who gave Jesus his coat. The family was warm and friendly. I had the feeling that I belonged among these good people at this time. I was able to relax. My apprehensions about making this trip were stilled. After greeting their mother and me, the married brothers went to their own homes for dinner.

As we ate, Jesus asked me about my occupation. His interest was obviously genuine and I became enthusiastic as I discussed shepherding to my gracious hosts. "Yes, I have been a shepherd all of my life. I love the outdoors and a shepherd has quiet times that allow him to think. I will admit that since your birth, Jesus, I have spent a great deal of time thinking about you. I suppose that became an obsession which brought me here. I am very glad that I made this trip."

I was watching the man in the coat made by my mother and trying to gauge his and Mary's reactions to my words. Jesus leaned forward, "Please tell me more about caring for sheep. A carpenter doesn't have the opportunity to learn about shepherding and I am quite interested in your occupation."

I could tell he was sincere and I hope I didn't overdo it. "A shepherd is almost like a parent to his sheep. You see my staff by the door. The crook at the end is useful to shepherds for many things. I can use my rod to strike at animals that approach our sheep. I can use the crook to rescue lambs when they manage to get caught in tangles or crevices. We love our sheep. Each sheep is special and the loss of even one sheep is emotionally stressful for a good shepherd. I have hired shepherds and they will tend to the sheep. However, a hired shepherd will not face severe danger for a single sheep. I have done just that on a number of occasions. Sheep are helpless—almost like little children—and become quite dependent upon their shepherd. Each sheep I ever tended soon came to recognize my voice and would come when I called. If they were unable for some reason to return, or to hear my voice, I would leave the flock in good hands and seek the lost sheep.

Not because of its monetary value, but because I love each sheep and care about every lamb. Even after years of shepherding, I still thrill at the sight of a newborn lamb. Because my father and his brother owned our flock, when one of us was required to be away from the sheep, we could leave knowing that the sheep were cared for by good shepherds who love each animal. The only time my entire family has left the sheep untended was that chilly night …" I stopped. I was about to say, "—when we saw the angels and went to the barn at the inn to see the baby." I remembered Jesus' request concerning his brothers and sisters. I finished lamely, "—was one night when there was an emergency and we had to leave them for a while."

Jesus said nothing. He was holding his bread and watching me intently with a concentration that relaxed me. He slowly took a bite of his bread and thought about my words. He finally said, slowly, "A good shepherd loves his sheep and cares about each sheep. I like that concept. It would be nice if more people had that attitude towards their fellow man, wouldn't it."

I knew this was not a question and did not attempt to answer it. Mary was smiling and watching her oldest son with admiration. The sisters were courteous but did not seem to hear my description of shepherding with the enthusiasm of their oldest brother. We ate in comfortable silence for a while.

As the women did the chores related to the meal clean up, Jesus suggested that we take a walk. While we walked, he thanked me for not revealing to his sisters his birth circumstances. He then added, "My time is not yet come. Yes, I do have a purpose in life and it is not building Herod's town of Sepphoris. I am still preparing for my life work. That time is approaching … and you will hear of me again." We walked slowly—going nowhere in particular. "You are thinking I came to bring peace into the world. I came to bring peace to people's hearts. You are thinking I came to rescue my people from the Romans. I came to rescue my people from themselves … from their own religious obsessions. The Jewish leaders have lost sight of my father's true desires. They have turned guidance into laws and turned the laws into innuendos and taken out the purpose of the laws, replacing that with fanatical lists of 'dos' and 'don'ts.' There is little concern for the human being, only the laws … everything seems to go back to the laws. Have you, David, studied the prophets?"

I began by telling him of the ridicule the shepherds received from the local religious leaders and of my disillusionment with the Synagogue. "To be honest with you, sir," I interjected, "I hate all of our Jewish leaders!" Then I told him that I began such studies after visiting Rabbi Bannus at Qumran. I told him about Rabbi Bannus and Rabbi Jacob and the Essenes. Jesus acknowledged that he knew of the group. He said he had a cousin who was an Essene and who was even now preaching a message of repentance in the valley around the Jordan River. "Is his name John?" I asked.

Jesus smiled, "Yes, I suppose you've met my cousin. Have you heard him preach? I hear he is attracting large audiences and performing many baptisms of repentance."

I was thinking aloud, "Actually, I didn't meet John. There were so many people around him after he finished preaching that I continued my journey to meet you. He is certainly a compelling preacher. Even Pharisees and Sadducees were among the audience when I heard John. There were far more peasants, but religious leaders were there. Some of *them* even accepted John's baptism of repentance. I can't picture those pompous, arrogant bastards seeing *themselves* as sinners! They're too busy looking down their noses on the rest of us."

We sat on the grass. I was so awed by his presence—and he did have an aura about him that was persuasive—that I waited for him to continue the conversation. Every time he spoke his words and demeanor had a gripping quality that inspired rapt attention. I can still accurately quote most of what he said. Again, in that quiet voice that compels you to listen carefully, he began to speak. "David, our nation was chosen from the time of Abraham. This elite status has led us into a comfortable religious arrogance. You are different. I think most laborers are closer to God than the people who are supposed to give them religious guidance. I, too, am a laborer. I spend my days with the working people of Israel. I know how they think and I understand their suffering—both at the hands of the Romans and at the hands of the leaders of our own religion. I fully understand your frustrations when your rabbi ridiculed you and the other shepherds about the angels. Our leaders have taken the attitude that only they have access to God. But you know from your own experience that God reaches out to the ordinary person. You know that God even reaches out to gentiles and to women. When my time comes, I will bear that message. But, David, that is not what the scribes and Pharisees want to hear. They hold political power because they have sold their souls to bind with Herod's sons and all that they represent."

There was nothing for me to say. From all that I knew, I realized that what he said was true. This province seemed so much less obsessed with religion than my home town that I had assumed the Galileeans were not caught up in the practices of those close to Jerusalem, the city with God's Temple and the High Priest.

The bright moon in the clear sky lit the sparkling eyes and shining hair. I looked at Jesus as he stared into the night sky. When his eyes fell on mine I felt strongly bonded to this young man. I knew that the savior was for real. That knowledge only filled my mind with questions. "You said your time has not yet come. Do you know when that time will be? And I get the strong impression that your mission in life is not to overthrow Rome."

"You are a wise man, David, shepherd of Bethlehem. Keep your eyes and ears open. Listen with your heart. Continue to study the prophets. There is much to learn from the great prophets of Israel and Judah. I cannot prepare you or others for my fulfillment of the prophecies. You can prepare yourself by studying and praying. You don't need to go to a synagogue or to the Temple to pray. God is listening to you wherever you are. My father is the God of love. His laws were made for the people. The laws of the lawyers, scribes, Sadducees and Pharisees are *their* laws because they no longer are for helping the people." He fell into silence again. I needed the silence to digest those words. He had referred to God as his father. That enhanced what we shepherds had been told by the angels the night Jesus was born. I wasn't sure where the deceased Joseph fit into the picture, but had already noticed that his brothers looked much like Joseph whereas Jesus and his two sisters favored their lovely mother. I repeated the words of the young man in my mind as we sat in the moonlight.

After a lengthy silence I said, "I believe I will return to Qumran and use the retreat of the Essenes to study the prophets. I will be alert for anything that signifies that your 'time has come.'"

Jesus stood and held out his hand to assist me as I rose to my feet. The touch of his hand was electrifying. There was nothing but the touch of his hand and yet it gave me the same overpowering sense of awe as I'd had on the night of the angels.

We returned to his house and after words of gratitude to the women for the meal and the cleanup I went to the room where I was to sleep as their guest. I wrapped myself in my robe and stretched out on my back. I continued to repeat the words of Jesus in my mind. I didn't want to forget a single word. I drifted into a deep sleep and woke, embarrassed at seeing that everyone else was up and busy. I went to the wash area and cleaned myself and shaved, changing into my clean clothes. The two brothers had stopped by for Jesus and were almost ready to return to Sepphoris so I ate alone. By this time my infatuation with Mary was a memory that gave me some pleasure, but her oldest son had become the obsession. I was not in awe in her presence nor was I giving any thought to the fact that she was a widow. My goals in life had changed. The first was to read and copy from the prophets. The second was to watch and wait for his 'time to come.'

9

I Leave Nazareth

After bidding farewell to the men as they went to work I again expressed my gratitude to the women for their kindness. As I was preparing to leave, one of Jesus' sisters took my waterskin to the well and filled it with cool water. Another sister was filling my wineskin while Mary was preparing bread and cheeses for me to take with me on my journey back. When I walked out of the house, Mary walked with me out of earshot of the daughters. "David, what are your plans? What did you and Jesus talk about? Don't tell me unless you are comfortable with it. After Joseph died I had no one to talk with about Jesus. I have treasured memories that reach back to the conception and into the present. One of them is your experience with the angels when Jesus was born. I would love to know anything you learned from him."

"Well," I began, "I am convinced that Jesus is the Son of God. Talking with him is captivating. He told me his 'time had not yet come.' He seemed to assume I'd know when he started his life work—which is not carpentry. He suggested that I study the prophets. I have been to the Essene community in the hills above the Dead Sea. It is called Qumran. They copy the scriptures there. The Essenes have made me a welcome guest any time I wish to visit. When I first visited there as a young man they believed me and my father when we told them about the angels. In fact, the leader of the group, Rabbi Bannus quoted scriptures which confirmed the events of your son's birth. The good rabbi has since died but the group is kind and will allow me to study the prophets as their guest. Jesus suggested that I study the prophets. So my current goal is to return to Qumran and do just that." Mary didn't respond and I knew she was doing what I had done the night before—she was trying to retain all that I had told her about my conversation with Jesus.

"David, you have been a blessing to me. Your fine parents are a wonderful memory. I was tired and trying to care for my son in very menial circumstances.

Your hospitality improved my recovery and made the long journey we had to take after leaving you bearable."

I thought about telling her about Herod's atrocities on the babies of Bethlehem. I hesitated and am glad I chose not to let her know about that. All it could accomplish would be to make her feel guilt for something that was not in any way of her making. I asked her if they came to Jerusalem for Passover each year. She said they came every year it was possible. I invited them to stay in my home at the next Passover.

Mary said they would not make plans for that because her oldest son made the decisions. I told her that if she remembered, I still lived in the same house and they were welcome to visit or to stay there. I was delighted when she said that was one of her most treasured memories and that she could find the house of David in Bethlehem. So we left it at that. She said they would watch for me at the Passover time. My coat that replaced the coat of Jesus was unlike most coats. Mother had woven in numerous colors with her nimble fingers. I wasn't difficult to find in a crowd. However, I was not in the habit of going to Passover. I now hated our Jewish leaders and our religion. However, if Jesus and Mary went to Passover, I would attend also. So with that promise I began my trek back down the mountain towards the Sea of Galilee.

10

Back to Qumran

I arrived at Jericho after taking the time to renew the friendships of my journey to Nazareth. At Tiberias I lingered with Josiah when he said Zebedee and his sons would be coming in within an hour or so. I could see their boat in the lake and they seemed to be pulling a heavy net in at that moment. So I waited, listening to Josiah and joining him for a cup of wine. I am not used to drinking much wine and had to be careful with the quantity. Josiah tried to ply me with more cups but I remembered the headache from my last visit with him and politely declined.

After almost two hours I could see the men pull in the nets and set sail for Josiah's fish market. I looked forward to chatting with these men again. They, in turn, were delighted to see me again because they were intensely interested in what I had learned and experienced in Nazareth. They had heard of Jesus, son of Joseph the carpenter, but were eager to hear every word that I could tell them first hand from my visit with Jesus and his family.

So, after pleasantries were exchanged, the fishermen gave rapt attention to my accounts of this storyteller from Nazareth. As I related to them that Jesus seemed very different from the rabbis of Bethlehem and the scribes and Pharisees in my area, these men heartily agreed that this would be a welcome change. In the course of the conversation—though it was not explicitly said—I gathered that they had little interest in our religion. I felt a sense of brotherhood with these religious rebels who would not be manipulated by the Jewish leadership. They wanted to know if I intended to return and issued me a warm welcome to be the guest in their home on my return trip. After our meal, I resumed my journey laden down with food and wine from my gracious friends. Josiah's wife Anna had even joined us while we ate and talked. She came out bringing fresh bread but quietly sat in the background, obviously enjoying the conversation with these fishermen and the shepherd with the Judean accent. So I departed light of heart and began my walk as I again repeated mentally the words of Jesus in order to fix them in my mind.

When I arrived at the desert area near the Jordan River where John had been preaching on my trip to Nazareth there was no sign of the prophet. There were still evidences of crowds having been there, but primarily due to the trampling. The area was cleaned of the detritus of human occupation. I continued my journey, still hoping to see the wild prophet who could attract even scribes and Pharisees to his message of repentance. I wanted to hear this man again—this time with the ears of a person who now knew that he was a cousin of the Son of God.

When I reached the area where I'd encountered the shepherds on my journey north, I listened for the bleating of sheep or the call of a shepherd to a lamb. I was rewarded and followed my ears to the area where the shepherds were grazing the sheep. They welcomed me enthusiastically. Their prime interest was in the man whose birth had been announced by angels to shepherds. It was exciting for me to be able to again recount the experiences I had in Nazareth. I found it very refreshing to be in the presence of men whom I understood perfectly and who accepted the strange story from a Bethlehem shepherd of an event almost three decades earlier. All of these experiences had been welling up in me and I was bursting with the desire to tell someone of the wondrous things that were simmering in Galilee.

I waited until the men had gotten the sheep settled for the night and I had bathed in the river and rested from the hot walk. We then sat in a circle around a fire, eating quail that I had killed with my slingshot. I shared my wine from my generous hosts in Tiberias. Since Jesus had told me that his siblings did not know of his miraculous birth events, I felt uncomfortable telling these men and boys about things that seemed confidential when Jesus told them to me. However, since I'd already told them about the angels, I saw no reason to keep that a secret. I withheld the information that he had said his "time had not come," and rather told them of the man. I readily told them that this Jesus is the Son of God—I had no doubt about that. I told them that he was currently a carpenter at Sepphoris but that he did plan to take action when the time was right for him. I assured them that I had no idea when that time would be, but that we would hear of Jesus of Nazareth again. I specified that I also had no idea what the action would be. I could, however, answer them that Jesus was not militant and would not be leading a Zealot army to expel the Romans. I recounted incidents surrounding my visit and told them about the marvelous storytelling skills of the carpenter from Nazareth. "You should see the children flock to him," I told them. "The man draws children like a mother hen draws her chicks to her. They adore him."

I told them the reason was obvious, he was extremely kind, he was gentle and he welcomed children. This is not done in our society. Children are supposed to stay out of the way and not interrupt or be present when adults are talking together. "Jesus loves the children and they know it," I told them. My final advice was to visit the prophet John and listen to his message of repentance. I told them that John was Jesus' cousin and that Jesus approved of what John was doing so it must be significant.

Being with my kind of people again was calming and in spite of—or perhaps because of—the sustained excitement of this entire trip, I went to sleep quickly and had to be awakened in the morning for our meal. I recognized the lamb that I had rescued—or rather he recognized me and came bleating to me with his mother close by. I scratched him on his soft head before resuming my journey to Jericho.

11

Jericho

The trip was uneventful. I continued repeating in my mind the words Jesus had said to me and rethinking the stories he told to the workmen and children in Sepphoris. Each time I rethought a story I sensed new insights and deeper meanings. I walked into Jericho eager to find Bartimaeus and tell him of my adventures. By this time I was familiar enough with Jericho and with my blind friend that I found him with relative ease. I called out his name and he came toward me eager to hear of my adventures with the man whose birth had been announced by angels—the Messiah who could give sight to the blind. We walked to his house where he had already prepared for my return by having wine, cheeses, figs and bread for us to eat while we talked. My pallet was clean and ready on the floor. I thought back to so many years ago when my father and I had befriended a blind boy with a long name. The big question in the mind of Bartimaeus was, "Is this the man whom the prophets say can heal the blind?" and he asked me that immediately after we entered his home.

"Bart," I began, "Jesus is the Son of God. Of that I have no doubt. He talked with me about 'his time' and I think was referring to when he would begin some sort of preaching tour or ministry. He has a cousin who is preaching in the wilderness around the Jordan in the northern area not far from Lake Galilee. I heard this young man preach. He is dynamic! There is something compelling about him. He spoke of one who would come after him. My theory is that Jesus is the one of whom he was speaking. Jesus never said this, but after spending time with Jesus, I feel he is the one prophesied by Isaiah of whom Rabbi Bannus spoke. When I leave Jericho, I intend to return to Qumran and study the prophets. Jesus suggested that I spend time becoming familiar with prophesies of the Messiah. He told me that I would hear of him again. I can't imagine him saying that unless he has plans to make a name for himself." I stopped. I had said much in those few words. I needed to give Bartimaeus time to contemplate what I had told him.

Bartemaeus, however, still had one thing on his mind. "Do you think he can heal a blind man?"

"Bart, you have made a good life for yourself. Of course being blind is a handicap and causes you to miss so much that we seeing people can enjoy. I need time to study the prophets and find out what they said about the blind being healed. I need to find out if I can tell when 'his time has come.' I want to research everything that might refer to the Prince of Peace. I will go from here to Qumran where the Essenes have told me I am always a welcome guest. There I will study and I will return and tell you what I learned. And yes, I will be especially watchful to see if the Messiah can heal the blind." I was afraid of giving false hope to the man and yet I also joined him in earnestly wishing that this Savior could also heal blindness of the eyes. From what Jesus had said I gathered that he was concerned about blindness of the souls of the Jewish leaders. If I hadn't seen the angels with my own eyes I'd never have encouraged Bartimaeus in the notion of ever seeing again. But—after seeing angels your faith in impossible miracles becomes viable.

When I awoke Bartimaeus was quietly preparing for our meal in the almost completely dark room. I almost said something before realizing that of course Bartimaeus did not need light. We had talked the night before in the light from the fire but lamps have no particular use in the home of a blind man who lives alone. However, when he heard me stirring, he lit a lamp he kept for visitors. Our morning meal was a quiet one. Both of us were immersed in thoughts of this man whom I had met. I wanted to learn everything I could about him and Bartimaeus wanted me to learn one particular thing about him. Bartimaeus walked with me to the edge of the city where Herod's fabulous palace still stood. I reached out and took his right hand in mine and clasped it, closing my left hand over our joined hands, and I promised to return to my friend with what I hoped was good news for him.

12

Qumran

I was tempted to enter the Dead Sea for that sensation of almost lying on top of water, but when I had done it with Father it had left my skin feeling slimy and itching so I resisted. The sun was painfully hot as I walked up the well beaten path to the community in these hills. The Essenes had retreated to an undesirable environment to ensure privacy and solitude as they did their work. I was hoping I would have the will to bear the intense heat and this arid land as I studied with the sect.

When I rounded the last curve of the winding path one of the women at a potter's wheel saw me and called out to announce my arrival. I felt self-conscious to be considered an honored guest with these devout people when I didn't even attend synagogue. As I entered the compound Rabbi Jacob was there with out-stretched hands to welcome me. All of the members wanted to hear of my encounter with the one announced to shepherds by angels. Rabbi Bannus had left his strong conviction that the two shepherds from Bethlehem had, indeed, been witnesses to the birth of the Messiah. So when I joined the men I assured them there was much to tell. They provided me with clean clothes and the women washed my dusty garments while I bathed. Only when we sat down to a meal did they begin to ask of my experiences on my journey. Uppermost in the questions: "Did you find Jesus of Nazareth?"

"Let me start at the beginning," I addressed the group. The women were allowed to stay for this recitation. "After leaving here I spent one night in Jericho with my blind friend and then headed north. In the wilderness near the Jordan I found a man preaching a message of repentance and mentioning one who would come after him. The crux of his message was for everyone to prepare the way for the Lord. He made references to the prophecies of Isaiah. That is where I want to start when I begin my studies here."

One of the men asked if this was a man named John and I told him yes. "He is a nazirite as were Samuel and Samson. A nazirite does not cut his hair. John's mother brought him here and he studied with us for a few years," he told me. "When he left us he said there was a work he had to do and he didn't expect to return. We have, of course, heard some word of the work of John the baptizer, but none of us has ever heard him preach. Did you hear his message?"

"I stopped to listen to him on my way to Nazareth. He preaches with powerful charisma. Many people were accepting his baptism of repentance. John preaches of preparing the way for the one who will come after him." I added, "After I met Jesus, he told me that John is his cousin. Jesus seemed to know about the work of John and approved of what he is doing."

"I have heard that John has offended some people," volunteered another man of the group. "When he was with us he impressed me as kind. He was extremely *intense* but not offensive."

"The way he preaches could easily offend the religious people where I come from," I assured them. "He called people snakes. I think this was directed at our Jewish leadership. Surprisingly this group did nothing to shut him up. Perhaps the very large number of John's followers was an effective deterrent to trying to stifle his message. Some of those being baptized by John were Jewish leaders but they were few.

"After hearing John I made my way to Tiberias where I met the owner of a fish market and two young fishermen with their father—all of whom became my friends. They had heard of Jesus of Nazareth but knew very little about him. They, too, asked me to report back to them on my return journey after meeting Jesus." I waited for questions but the audience was waiting in rapt attention to hear of my experiences in Nazareth.

"When I arrived in Nazareth I found a town of friendly people and an innkeeper who seemed to know all about everyone in Nazareth. He directed me to the home of Jesus and his widowed mother Mary. Because the men were away at work at the construction site in Sepphoris, I decided to wait and not intrude on the women nor try to meet Jesus immediately after a day of work. The innkeeper, James, told me that Jesus was the only unmarried son and still lived with his mother along with two sisters. So I spent the night in Nazareth and in the morning joined the workmen as they walked to Sepphoris for their day's work." Telling the story brought back the memories that were so deeply impressed in my mind. I could feel my pulse quicken as I approached the point where I saw and recognized Jesus because of the coat he was wearing. "I wandered around the building site looking for a man I did not know on sight. But, because of the gift I had given the holy family on that day that the magi gave gifts, I knew that I had found the Prince of Peace when I saw a young man wearing the seamless coat my mother had made. My mother Martha was an expert on combing, spinning, dyeing and weaving wool. The coat she had made for me had no seams because she had skillfully woven the sleeves into the body of the coat. And Mother had chosen more expensive dyes for this cloak she was weaving her only child—a son whom she loved very much. There is no coat in Israel that is finer than the coat worn by Jesus of Nazareth." I had managed to go off on a tangent when I thought of my mother, the coat, and the magi.

I pulled my mind back to the story the Essenes were waiting to hear: "Jesus was working as a carpenter. When Jesus was born, his father Joseph's occupation was carpentry. Jesus attracted a crowd wherever he went. Even children flocked to hear the stories from this handsome young man during their breaks from work." Again I ceased concentrating on the story and my audience and envisioned the face of the storyteller as he told a story about olive trees. I was seeing that face and the visages of the rapt audience when one of the women surprised herself and the men by asking me to continue.

I laughed this time. "Meeting Jesus and hearing him tell his stories has left a deep impression on me. I find myself rethinking things he said and trying to keep his words exact in my mind. You will find that I retreat into these memories all along. I appreciate it when you jolt me back to the present." I then had to think where I had left off—oh yes, the storyteller—"Jesus met with me after the break and asked me not to tell his siblings of the miraculous events I had witnessed at his birth. I told all of this to you long ago so you already know. This is the man you are awaiting. Jesus is the Messiah. Another confidential thing Jesus told me was that 'his time had not yet come' and that I would hear of him again. He referred to his father as a god of love. This leads me to believe that he will begin some sort of ministry when the time is right. Listen to this because I found it to be the most intense thing he had to say. Jesus said, 'You are thinking I came to bring peace into the world. I came to bring peace to people's hearts. You are thinking I came to rescue my people from the Romans. I came to rescue my people from themselves ... from their own religious obsessions. The Jewish leaders have lost sight of my father's true desires." They have turned guidance into laws and turned the laws into innuendos and taken out the purpose of the laws, replacing that with fanatical lists of 'dos' and 'don'ts.' There is little concern for the human being, only the laws ... everything seems to go back to the laws. Have you, David, studied the prophets?' I believe this is almost word for word what he told me when we were talking privately. So here I am, eager to study the prophets."

"You mentioned Jesus making a reference to his father as a god of love. Did this carpenter Joseph claim to be God?" This came from one of the scribes.

"On that night of Jesus' birth the angels announced the birth of the Savior of the world. Later Mary confided in me that her son is the Son of God. I am certain that Jesus was referring to Yahweh when he talked of his father's plans for him. It is still a mystery to me, but Jesus is the Son of God."

The rabbi then spoke, "Yes, you are right. And it is good that you want to study the prophets. Brother Simon, you were pointing out some text in Isaiah's prophecy to me just last week. I believe this was about the subject we are discussing."

Brother Simon went to his copy table and picked up an unfinished scroll. Handling it with great care, he quickly found what he was seeking. Simon began to read from it: "Behold a virgin shall conceive and bear a son and his name will be Immanuel—*God with us.*" No one spoke.

The silence lasted for several minutes. No one wanted to break the spell that had come over us. The great prophet Isaiah was speaking to us from the past. Finally Rabbi Jacob announced that we would continue discussions each evening after my day of studying the prophecies. I looked forward to the studies and to the conversations and the insights of these scholars after our evening meal. I returned to my same cave as I'd used for sleeping on the previous visit. Even Brother Asher's snoring could not disturb my sleep on this night. I lay on my back again mentally repeating the words of Jesus. Tomorrow I would write them down to ensure that I would never forget them.

13

Studying the Prophets

Shepherds rise early and have long days. However, these Essenes have taught me a great deal about long days. They rise to pray before dawn and begin their tasks after morning devotions followed by a late morning meal. Rabbi Jacob brought me the first scroll of the prophet Isaiah. I requested pen and ink and offered to buy a skin for my notes but the group would not let me pay for anything. They assured me that my presence and my sharing of what I learned were of immeasurable value to them.

Because Rabbi Bannus had first consulted the Isaiah scroll, that was my first request. So on my first day I read from Isaiah for the entire day. I reread passages and put grass stalks in the scroll where I wanted to study more carefully. Many things were falling into place. I found it amazing how much was obvious and how much more was there if I read and concentrated on various passages. My eyes were tired but my heart elated as I began to copy the very special sections of the prophet Isaiah which I found linked with Jesus or with his cousin John and his message.

Noting the perfect script of the Essene copiers, I meticulously copied certain sentences and phrases: "… the future will bring honor to this region … even to Galilee itself. The people who walked in darkness have seen a great light … you have given them great joy Lord; you have made them happy … you have broken the yoke that burdened them … you have defeated the nation that oppressed and exploited your people … A day is coming when human pride will be ended and human arrogance destroyed. Then the Lord alone will be exalted." (Is. 9) As I read these words again and again, the words of Jesus were in my mind: "You are thinking I came to bring peace into the world. I came to bring peace to people's hearts. You are thinking I came to rescue my people from the Romans. I came to rescue my people from themselves … from their own religious obsessions. The Jewish leaders have lost sight of my father's true desires."

Isaiah had written: "*A child is born to us! A son is given to us!* He will be called, 'Wonderful Counselor, Mighty God, Eternal Father, and *Prince of Peace*.' His royal power will continue to grow; his kingdom will always be at peace. He will rule as King David's successor, basing his power on right and justice, from now until the end of time." I read on and then carefully copied: "The royal line of David is like a tree that has been cut down … the spirit of the Lord will give him wisdom and the knowledge and skill to rule his people … he will defend the rights of the helpless … he will judge the poor fairly." (Is. 11) The man from Nazareth had spoken words that assured me that he was the Messiah. He fit the requirements of the man described by Isaiah and he descended from my ancestor David, for whom I was named.

I stopped writing. My mind was overcome with so much information and the effort of struggling to see the prophecy of Isaiah fulfilled in Jesus. I copied for Bartemaeus: "When that day comes, the deaf will be able to hear a book being read aloud, and the blind, who have been living in darkness, will open their eyes and see. Poor and humble people will once again find the happiness which the Lord, the holy God of Israel, gives. It will be the end of those who oppress others and show contempt for God." When I had read this passage several times I stopped reading and attempted to configure in my mind which people Jesus saw as the oppressors. Was it the Romans? Was it our own religious leaders? Was it a combination of these people? I was aware that poor and humble people were neither the Romans nor the Jewish leaders. I also reminded myself, as I often had, that Jesus' birth was announced only to shepherds and to gentiles.

As I read, "A voice cries out, 'Prepare in the wilderness a road for the Lord! Clear the way in the desert for our God!" I remembered those very words. They had been shouted across a barren wilderness area near the Jordan River by Jesus' cousin John. This confirmed again that I had indeed witnessed the birth of the Messiah and had met the man who would save his people. But, as Jesus had said, what he was to save them *from* was not what they were expecting. So, as priests, Levites, rabbis, Pharisees and Sadducees waited for a royal king, a quiet man was biding his time in Nazareth waiting for the time when his father would signal him to fulfill his purpose on earth. I was finding in these prophecies that his purpose was at odds with our religious leaders. And, after all, Jesus himself had told me that in so many words.

I spent the rest of the day studying Isaiah. Tomorrow I would use other scrolls but Isaiah had clinched it all in my mind. Here I was—a lowly shepherd—a man who had been invited to experience the wonder of God Incarnate. Almighty God had allowed shepherds and eastern magi to witness the birth of His own son.

Yahweh had come to earth in the form of a human born to a simple couple from Nazareth a beautiful young woman and her carpenter husband. I, David had met this carpenter's son as a young man, now also a carpenter, quietly waiting for "his time" to come—a time in which he said I would hear of him again.

I spent three weeks among these humble people—reveling in their treasure trove of scriptures and being treated as an honored guest. When I had copied and memorized much of what they were vigilantly preserving with their neatly written scrolls carefully stored in caves in this wilderness near the Dead Sea, I prepared to take my leave.

"David, you are a bachelor." The rabbi reminded me. "We invite you to join us as we continue our work. We, too, are waiting for the Messiah to make his move." These words tempted me. Maybe this is God's plan for me. I waited several minutes before answering the godly scholar. The silence was not uncomfortable. These people had waited patiently for years—most through their adult lifetimes—for this man whom I had met. I needed to give intense consideration to Rabbi Jacob's proposal. Was this my role in life?

"Rabbi Jacob, I believe my mission is not the same as yours," I began. "Jesus told me I would hear of him again. If I stay here I will be isolated from the activities of Israel. I believe my role is to be there when Jesus begins his ministry. I think I have a call to somehow participate in this ministry. Jesus is not like the rabbis, priests and other religious leaders. He has told me his ministry will be different from what they are doing. I want to be a part of it. I have learned so much with you good people. There is no way I can thank you enough for what you have meant to me but I feel I must go back to Bethlehem and wait."

Rabbi Jacob put his hands on my shoulders. "David, will you return to us and keep us aware when the Messiah emerges from his role as Jesus the carpenter of Nazareth?"

"Sir, I will do my best. When Isaiah says the eyes of the blind will be opened, I wonder if he means literally. Jesus said the peace was to be in our hearts. I wonder if the blindness to be healed is in our hearts. My friend Bartemaeus, who visited here with me, certainly hopes Jesus means literally. And when Jesus begins his ministry, I want to take him to Bartemaeus. I believe that Jesus will bring light to his soul if not to his eyes. And, yes, I will surely return to share the good news with you, my friends."

I turned to walk away. I loved these people who had been so good to me and was ashamed to cry at our parting. I didn't hurry, but raised my hand in a farewell gesture as I rounded the path down from the hills and disappeared from their sight.

14

Waiting

I stopped in Jericho as I had promised Bart. As I walked through the streets of this bustling city, I thought of the day many years ago when I, a very young man, had met the blind boy. At the time I would have never guessed that in the first short meeting I had made a friend for life. Bart was at home and I announced myself at his doorway. "David, come in, come in! I have been waiting for you for days. You must have found much to study."

I laughed, "Well, the Essenes are so hospitable and their presence so refreshing that I found it hard to leave. Besides they are good cooks. However, I will deign to eat your cooking to show that I am still a humble man."

Bartimaeus laughed heartily. "You can eat my food or go hungry, you rascal. I've been saving my best cheese and wine for you for days."

We exchanged friendly jibes. However, the blind man was not patient enough to wait for me to get ready to tell him about the prophecies of a man who could heal blindness. "David, what do the prophets say about the miracle worker? I remember hearing of one who could heal the blind. Did you find that in your studies?"

I suppose I didn't have the faith of the blind man from Jericho because I was hedging my answer. "Bart, Isaiah does make a number of references to the deaf hearing and the mute speaking. There is a passage about the lame leaping for joy. While I was with Jesus he talked of peace as symbolic—that is, that he would bring peace to our hearts. For your sake, I sincerely hope the references to healing the blind are not just symbolic. However, I would be deceiving you if I did not tell you that it is possible this scripture is also symbolic. I can say that if you meet Jesus, you will not be disappointed whether he heals your eyes or your soul and your hopes. He is the Messiah and I am confident that an encounter with him would leave you with either healing of the eyes or of your hopes."

This was not the answer that Bartimaeus had wanted to hear but he trusted me and wanted to find solace in my words—discouraging as they were—if the truth be told. "David, if God can send angels announce his arrival, don't you think God could give his son the power to literally heal blindness?"

He waited patiently while I chewed on these words. I was so afraid of giving him false hopes. "Yes, Bartemaeus, yes, I think the Messiah could literally bring sight to the blind if he truly wanted to. I shall pray that you will meet Jesus of Nazareth and that he will restore your sight." I thought about my words as they hung in the dark room. "You also should pray for healing from the Messiah. He told me that God listens to our prayers. And Jesus says we do not have to go to a synagogue nor the Temple to pray. Jesus says our prayers are heard wherever we speak them. Yes, Bartemaeus, let's anticipate healing."

We prayed before eating. Jesus had led prayers before eating but in my family we did not pray before we ate. But Jesus had said that God hears our prayers—and we both had things to pray about. We each had much to think about. As I tried to sleep I heard the whispered prayers from the adjacent room. I could not hear the words, but I knew the gist of the prayer. I was praying the same prayer. After a night's rest I took my shepherd's crook, my scrolls, slingshot, my small bundle of clothes, and gave the parcel of food from the Essenes to Bart. When I clasped the hand of my friend and looked into those clouded eyes I felt tears rolling down my face and was glad Bart could not see this. He put his left hand on my shoulder and asked that I continue to pray for him to find the Savior, who could give sight to the blind. I gripped his hand and nodded, as if he could see me, embarrassed that my voice would betray my tears. Yes, I would pray for my friend.

When I passed through Bethany I walked past the home of Martha, Mary and Lazarus, hoping to be rewarded by seeing the vivacious Martha. The wish in my heart was fulfilled. In the yard the dreamy Mary was again in the swing. This must be something which she does frequently because when I first saw her she was in the same swing and singing in the same lovely voice. And, my good fortune was afire today because Martha was in the doorway applying adobe to the wall near the frame where the dried mud was crumbling. Since Martha was doing a man's job, I assumed Lazarus was not at home. He was a young man so he was probably at his job earning the household income. I did not enter the premises but called over to Martha. "Madam, Madam, could I help you with that chore? I am a shepherd but as a boy I added a room to our house. I think I can still do this work."

Martha looked up and seeing a stranger was hesitant. "I can do this. I have done it before!" she called back.

I did not want to be presumptuous or forward, but neither did I want to miss this opportunity to meet the lady of whom I dreamed. "I am much taller than you. I will not enter your home, but I can help where you cannot reach!"

"Thank you, shepherd-housebuilder. Perhaps I could use the help of a taller person, at that." Martha's voice did not have the soft melodic timbre of her younger sister, but it was music to my ears. She spoke with more authority and self assurance. I restrained myself so as not to become too aggressively friendly with this family whom I knew, in a way, but who did not know me at all. I walked to the pretty lady and took the trowel as she offered it to me.

"Actually, it is obvious that you know what you are doing," I offered. Your masonry is indeed quite nice."

Mary stopped swinging but continued singing as she watched the two of us. I worked my way up the wall listening to her melodious psalm. Martha tried to make conversation, "My sister sings beautifully, doesn't she," she remarked. Then she added, "However, I would not want her repairing our house." With that both of us laughed. Mary, who had heard her sister's remarks, continued singing, acknowledging her own skills by demonstration. Martha was a very attractive woman but without the fragile delicacy of her sister Mary. Martha's eyes flashed with emotion when she talked and her thick wavy hair did not have the fine thinness of her sister's long dark brown hair. Martha's mouth readily broke into a smile and there were wrinkles at the corners of her eyes as if she smiled a lot. Mary's face was paler than her sister's. I presume sitting under a tree singing does not tan the skin as much as doing chores and cooking. I even wondered if the fragile Mary went to the well for water.

My palms began to sweat, making the trowel want to slip in my hands. I had not felt quite like this since the almost thirty years ago when I attended the birth of a baby whose mother was the most beautiful woman I'd ever seen. It was a relief to have overcome or outgrown my passion for Mary, the mother of Jesus. However, my current passion was difficult to hide—or at least I greatly feared that was the case. As I turned back to my work, grasping the trowel tightly, I felt my face redden.

Had Martha seen that? She spoke again and her voice seemed to betray just that, "Shepherd, what is your name?" she asked.

"I am David, son of Joshua, shepherd of Bethlehem," I replied.

"Well, David, my name is Martha and this musician here is my sister Mary," Martha replied. "We have a brother, Lazarus, who is at work. He is a tinsmith and sells his wares in Jerusalem. We expect him home in another hour." I was wondering if lovely Martha feared me and was sounding a warning but she allayed these thoughts by adding, "Perhaps you could join us for supper after our brother returns. We are grateful for your help with the wall. Your height does give you a distinct advantage over me when it comes to chores such as these."

I was ecstatic! "I would be honored to join the family of Martha, Mary and Lazarus for dinner," I quickly agreed. Then, wondering what to do for the next hour flashed into my mind. "I need to find a place to bathe. I am returning to Bethlehem from Jericho and have had a long hot walk." My time with the Essenes had instilled in me an obsession with cleanliness and I could not enter a home after my hot, dusty journey. And I was absolutely horrified at the thought of this beautiful lady kneeling at my feet to wash them.

Martha directed me to the creek near town and I took leave of the two ladies and walked the half mile to the stream to get presentable. Here was a lady I wanted to impress and having dinner in these dusty clothes would not the memory I wanted to leave with spirited Martha. I found the water and followed the stream to a private area where I bathed and changed into clean clothes that the Essenes had laundered for me.

Clean and wearing fresh clothes, I returned to the well in Bethany and watched for the young man I knew to be Lazarus to return from Jerusalem. I washed my feet again at the well because I was determined that Martha would not have any reason to perform this customary act of hospitality. After seeing Lazarus pass on his way home, I walked to the home I had just helped repair. When I arrived I saw Martha showing Lazarus my work and although out of earshot could hear the word 'David' a couple of times. I waited until this conversation was over to approach.

Not only was Martha a good mason; she was a superb cook. I had expected very plain food and was surprised that in the hour since I had left, the talented young woman had prepared a feast by my standards. Mutton was on the menu. Perhaps she had chosen this dish because I was a shepherd. In any case, the seasonings were exquisite. My mother was the best weaver in the area, but Martha's cooking skills surpassed those on which I had been reared. Mary was very quiet and introspective. Lazarus seemed to be probing me excessively. He wanted to know about my parents, my background, my journey, and my livelihood. I hoped his inquisitiveness was instigated by an interest Martha had shown in me when she was telling her brother about me. When Lazarus or I spoke Martha's dark eyes danced from one of us to the other. I was grateful that the women ate with us, making the occasion informal and friendly. I'm sure that with two sisters and a brother, it was perfectly normal for the three to eat together. I was relieved that my presence did not change that. It gave me the sensation that perhaps I was considered a friend and accepted as if I were a member of the family. I took the time to tell the family some of the experiences I had but did not repeat the story of the angels. I was comfortable telling other shepherds about that—and the Essenes. I was not at ease sharing this with strangers—especially not to a woman I wanted to impress. Having her think I was possibly insane was not what I wanted her to remember about me.

After the meal the family wanted to discuss the visit I'd had with the Essenes. They had heard of these devout people and wanted to know more about them. After telling them about the scholarly work of the Essenes and their mission of awaiting the Messiah, I told them that this group thought Jesus was the Messiah. I gave some of the scripture passages that reinforced this belief. All three of them were obviously very interested. Lazarus then said that his family was not actively involved in the synagogue. Of course they went to Jerusalem for Passover and followed the prescribed rituals of purification and sacrifice for the annual occasion, but they were uncomfortable with the demands of the High Priest and his followers. I sighed with relief at this and stated that I, too, had become disillusioned with Judaism when I was in my late teens. I added that from my conversation with Jesus, I felt that he, too, was not happy with the direction our religious leaders were taking us Jews and that he had shared that with me. As I was leaving, Lazarus invited me to return for another visit. I glanced at Martha and she smiled warmly, blushing under my gaze. I readily accepted and the date was set.

When I reached Bethlehem it was dark and I went directly to my home. Uncle Nathan's son had been caring for my house so when I arrived everything was in order. I went to bed and dreamed about vivacious Martha.

In the morning I made my way to Aunt Ruth's house. She was already hard at work on her baskets. Her hands were gnarled and calloused from this weaving of thousands of baskets over the years. She told me that my uncle and his sons were with the sheep in the south pasture. I told her about my adventures after which we shared lunch. Aunt Ruth discussed her husband with me. "Your uncle is too old to be out there caring for sheep. David, our sons are unable to do all of the work now needed to care for the sheep. Their sons are still too young to be able to assume full responsibility. We need you." I had been so busy with my own pursuits I hadn't noticed this and felt bad. "If you can assume full responsibility for only a year or two we should have grandsons to take over from then on."

"Aunt Ruth, you know I can help if you need me. I'll go and send your husband home. And you can count on me as long as you need me. You know that." With that I left her and headed for the south pasture where I would find my uncle and his sheep. As much as I wanted to get married, I also had asked a lot from my family and owed it to them to help until I was no longer needed.

As I approached the flock of my uncle he recognized me from a great distance—by my gait, I'm sure, because Uncle Nathan's eyesight was that of an old man. He came to meet me, welcoming me warmly and assuring me that I would always have a job in Bethlehem as a shepherd. When I told him that his wife wanted him to come home he laughed. "That woman wants to run my life," he said. However, he added, "but I sure have missed her. Because of the drought we have had to come to this pasture far from Bethlehem. It's been two weeks since I was home. I will leave in the morning after you have been introduced to our new lambs." Since I had been gone during lambing season, it was important that the new members of the flock recognize my voice as their protector.

I spent the winter with the sheep. Since I had no family, there was no reason for me to spend time at home. Of course, I was going to Bethany whenever I was invited. Before winter was over I almost felt like a member of that family. However, Martha was not family—she was an attractive, charming and talented young woman who was winning the heart of David the shepherd of Bethlehem. When I was in the fields and the sheep were resting nearby, I would visualize the dark eyes darting glances at me. I could see her blush when our eyes met. I dreamed of her frying bread with droplets of perspiration trickling down her face and her glances at me with a broad smile showing white even teeth on her tanned face. I could hear her sharp voice calling out to Mary for help and then hear her soft gentle voice as she asked me to come again. I saw in my mind her hand brushing her long dark hair back behind her ears as it fell forward when she was toiling. I delighted in the memory of her with the trowel tiptoeing as she reached for the upper corner of the doorway. And my pulse quickened as I recalled looking down into her face as I replaced the broken stucco with ease.

Once when I was visiting with Martha, Lazarus and Mary, they told me that they had heard of John and his preaching in the wilderness. They had also heard that he was making converts, but that he was also making enemies. Many of the Sanhedrin were angry with him but they were also afraid of him because of his large following. However, he had also angered Herod Antipas, tetrarch of Galilee, who is not a man one wants as an enemy. John had openly criticized Herod for marrying his brother Philip's wife Herodias. The Pharisees and Sadducees, whom John was openly criticizing, were glad to see him angering Herod. This might solve their problem of what to do with this outspoken man with a great following and powerful charisma.

15

I Return to Nazareth

It had been a year and a half since my visit to Nazareth. I had studied the prophets and memorized many passages. The prophet Micah had said that the little village of Bethlehem would be the birthplace of the Redeemer. I knew that Jesus was the Messiah. This awareness created a growing restlessness in me. I discussed with Uncle Nathan another trip to Nazareth. If, as Jesus had put it, his 'time had *not* come,' then I would at least have the pleasure of visiting with the family again. Uncle Nathan assured me that his grandsons were ready to completely take over and that I was no longer needed to ensure the safety of the sheep. I, of course, knew that. I had spent the past months with them and had helped train them and watched them grow up.

I visited with friends in Bethlehem and Martha in Bethany. I promised Martha that I would see her as soon as I returned. I really wanted to ask this lady to marry me but this unfulfilled spot in my heart would not allow me to settle down. I made preparations to depart. Bethany would be my first stop. I would visit Bartimaeus both coming and returning, but would plan to return to Qumran only after my visit in Nazareth, hoping I would have some news to share with my Essene friends. I also hoped to visit with the shepherds near the Jordan. Perhaps I would hear the charismatic preacher John shouting his message of repentance. As always, I carried my shepherd's crook and my slingshot. When I was tending the sheep I would entertain myself honing my skills with the slingshot. And I found that I could still successfully kill or drive off a predator. My cousins and nephews never acquired the dexterity I had mastered with the slingshot. It felt good as these young men—boys, almost—looked with admiration at their uncle almost fifty years old. Their parents had raised them to respect their elders, but the undisguised admiration for my skills was a real ego booster. So, again traveling as a man of little means with my money hidden in a false patch on my waterskin, I departed early one spring morning to return to Nazareth and try to see Jesus again.

The trip to Jericho was uneventful. I encountered a small band of Roman soldiers and was reassured of my safety by their presence. I walked to Bartemaeus' home only to find it empty. I decided to go to the well and refill my water and then wait for my blind friend to return. I was lounging near his doorway, sitting in the shade of the house when I was awakened by none other than Bart stumbling on my legs. He regained his balance. I yelped in surprise. "David, are you trying to break my neck!" he asked. Then he laughed heartily.

"How did you know it was me?" I asked.

"You shouted. I know your voice. Come in, come in," Bart offered. He went next door for fire to light the lamp he kept for visitors. The weather was pleasant and we sat outside for a while before darkness fell. I was surprised that he could tell the time of day by stepping out into the sunlight. As the sun fell behind the hills Bartimaeus was preparing food for the two of us. I quickly presented the food I had brought. I had learned that there was a certain goat cheese that he truly enjoyed so I made sure I brought a large bag of that cheese.

As we had supper Bart asked if I was planning to return to Nazareth. "Yes, my friend. I have been thinking about Jesus for eighteen months and I must go and visit him again. Because he told me that I would hear of him again, I have not made this trip but I cannot continue to wait. He is at the prime of life. I would think it is time for him to begin fulfilling all that the prophets said of him. Much of it I don't fully understand but I want to learn all I can from him. His mother is very beautiful and I enjoy seeing her also." I was embarrassed that I had made a reference to "seeing"—especially to seeing someone who is beautiful. I hesitated; he didn't show offense in his face or demeanor. "I will leave tomorrow for the walk to Lake Galilee. After my visit I will return and tell you what I have learned."

"David, will you ask him if he can heal the blind, as it says in the prophets? Please ask him if he can give sight to someone who has never seen anything except darkness since the day he was born. The priests consider me unclean. They blame my blindness on me even though I was born with it." I looked on my friend's face and my hatred for the priests flared.

I looked at those almost white eyes and, in spite of my experiences with Jesus, doubted that these eyes would ever see. What do I tell a man who is building such an impossible hope? "Bart," I commented, "I will tell Jesus about you. If he has begun his work, I will even come back and take you to Galilee if necessary. Please pray that I will find Jesus again. He seemed to promise that I would when I last saw him. I will do all that I can for you."

Bartimaeus accepted this answer. He even smiled. This man had greater faith in the impossible than I did and I felt ashamed. I had read the prophets but I had also talked with Jesus who indicated that his mission was to the heart and soul of man more than to the body.

The following morning Bart walked with me for about two miles. He was carrying a cane, which he seldom used. He was not familiar with the road after the first mile and needed this for his return. I urged him to come no farther because of wild animals as we left the perimeter of habitation in Jericho. There were shepherds near the outskirts of town, traveling to find greener pastures. I hugged my blind friend and waved to the shepherds. They saw my crook and knew that I was one of them.

I traveled along the Jordan, as before. All was silent, but for the splashing of the river over rocks as it raced towards the Dead Sea. I was able to relax and think about what I was hoping to find on this journey. There had been a drenching rain during the night and the walk was pleasant without dust and insects. I suppose I was feeling my age, for several times I chose to sit on a stone or log by the river and relax. When I reached the area where I'd seen the shepherds, there was no sign of them. Across the river I could see swine grazing with their gentile owners tending them. I was grateful to be Jewish as I could not imagine tending such noisy, dirty animals that appeared to love the mud. Sheep are trusting, gentle and quiet. The occasional bleats are generally lambs and ewes calling out to one another. I could also recognize bleats which signified danger approaching, of course.

As I drew nearer to Tiberias, I saw mobs of people facing a man on a hill. Although he was too far away for me to recognize him, I knew this would be John the baptizer. He was still drawing large crowds and I again saw a few of the well dressed Jewish leaders that I had seen on my first trip. This time I wanted to hear the message of the cousin of Jesus. I had to circle the crowd and come up almost behind John to hear what he was saying, even though he was shouting. He did not attract children as had Jesus. His audience consisted of mostly men though there was a smattering of women in the audience. When I was able to hear his words the message was basically the same. He was calling for repentance from sin. As I listened I thought about sin. What are my sins? I have rebelled against the synagogue, but Jesus hadn't given me the impression that he considered this a sin. I had long since ceased to feel lust for beautiful Mary. I had cared for my parents; I had studied the prophets, memorizing many sections which referred to the Messiah. Perhaps my sin was my intense hatred of the Jewish leaders or my lack of faith in Jesus. Bartemaeus, a blind man who had never met Jesus had more faith in his miraculous powers than I, who had talked with the Son of God, did. But Jesus, though the Son of God, was a man. Jesus was born the same way I was. Well, the circumstances were certainly different, but he entered the world as a human. The angels seemed more godlike than this personable man with whom I had discussed religion. Maybe I needed the faith of blind Bart. I listened intently as John referred to the one who was to come after him. Isaiah had written about the "voice in the wilderness" and John was surely that voice. Jesus had to be the fulfillment of this prophecy. I kept asking myself if I needed to repent in order to be acceptable to Jesus. If John was not good enough to tie his shoes, I surely could not be worthy to visit in his home. Yet I hesitated to repent because I could not put my finger on my sins. Perhaps that, in itself, *was* my sin. When John began his baptisms I watched these people walk out of the Jordan almost radiant with a sense of relief from their experience. As the crowd melted away, I joined the ones who trekked towards Tiberias.

16

Tiberias

It was late afternoon when I arrived at Josiah's dock. I looked out into the lake for the boat of Zechariah and his sons but the only boats on the lake appeared to be those transporting a few people across the water between Capernaum and Tiberias. I went to the inn and found friends there who remembered me. Again they enjoyed listening to my accent. There were several Roman soldiers in the inn and the area around them was abandoned. I suppose the Romans didn't really enjoy our company any more than we did theirs. If a soldier demands your seat, you don't question the order but just obey it. However, these people of Galilee did not seem to have the awe of the Roman iron fist that Judean Jews seemed to have. There was even some friendly banter crossing the room between Jews and Romans.

My previous experience with the inn led me to simply go to the pier and prepare for my night's rest. I was able to bathe in the lake after dark. I rolled up my clothing bundle for a pillow for my head and used my cloak as a blanket as the cool of evening dispelled the heat of the day. In spite of my excitement at being near Nazareth, I slept soundly. I was awakened by Josiah's loud laughter when he found me asleep after dawn. "Well, you lazy rascal, I see you are back. You had to come all the way from Bethlehem to find a good fish dinner! Am I right!?"

After recovering from the shock of being awakened from a sound sleep I was able to laugh with my tormentor. "Josiah, it is good to see you again. Yes, of course I made this journey to eat your cooking. Perhaps I'll even get the strength from that to do a few other things while I am here."

The man laughed generously at my attempt at a humorous response. He quickly scaled and filleted a fish and began heating his pan of oil for cooking it. To tell the truth, there was a little bit of truth in what he said. I have never had fish as good as that cooked by my large red-haired friend in Tiberias. As he cooked he began chattering. I found what he had to say immensely interesting. "Your friend, Jesus of Nazareth has visited us," he began. I hung on every word.

"He is certainly an interesting and pleasant fellow. He was here about two months ago and spent some time with Zebedee and his sons. I tried to listen to all he had to say but I had to attend to the fish and missed much of the conversation. I think you might like to watch their boat across the lake and return when Zebedee comes in with his catch. He and his sons spent a long time with this Jesus. They even took him out in their boat. He was intensely interested in their profession." I remembered my conversation with Jesus in which we had discussed my occupation. His interest had certainly appeared to be genuine. I don't suppose he intends to change occupations to shepherding or fishing, but instead is just a remarkably good conversationalist who learns from others by asking and listening. I walked out on the pier and watched the boat for a while. Fishing didn't look as if it was going well. I didn't see them pulling in nets. Having never been in a boat, I wondered if it would be scary. One thing was certain: I didn't know how to swim. Would Jesus know how to swim, growing up in a mountain village?

So I walked out onto the pier and waited. Josiah called out to me as he went to his home. He'd salted down all of his fish and there was no activity so he chose to take leave of his work for a while. I'm sure if I'd stayed nearby he'd have continued to chat.

Late in the afternoon the boat began to approach the pier. Josiah saw them coming and returned. He commented to me as I walked back to his work area that there wouldn't be many fish today. He had been watching his favorite fishermen and didn't see any signs that they were having a successful day. I went back out on the pier and watched the sun slide below the mountains to the west. The chill seemed to be almost immediate. I put on my cloak and waited for the fishing boat.

As the men arrived I could see in their tired faces that Josiah was right about the fishing. However, when they recognized me they quickly brightened. The youngest son, John, called out to me, "David, shepherd of Bethlehem, it's great to see you again. We've met your friend from Nazareth. We invite you to join us for supper and stay the night in our home. There is much to talk about."

This was an invitation that I readily accepted. Visiting with these nice people would, in itself, be a great experience, but since they had met Jesus I was eager to hear what he had said to them and what their reactions were to the man born King of the Jews. So, as they disembarked I thanked them for the invitation and agreed to their hospitality. Josiah did not jest with them about their small catch. This was not a point of humor. These men depended on fishing as their livelihood.

17

In Zebedee's Home

I walked with Zebedee through streets along the shoreline until we reached his house in the little village of Magdala. Neither son was married so they still lived with their parents. Their mother, Salome, gave me a warm welcome. I had bathed in the lake while the sun was high in the sky and didn't even need dust to be washed from my feet. Joanna went to get the water for this but I stopped her, realizing that the men of the family had spent their day on a boat and also didn't need their feet washed. I didn't need her to do this for me. She showed me to a place near the fire where I could put my belongings and later sleep.

Although I was eager to hear the men's impressions of Jesus, and hoping they would remember his exact words as I had, I waited for their tiredness and disappointment in their bad fishing day to dissipate. I felt it was best to let them initiate the conversation. They would already know that I was eager to learn of their time with Jesus of Nazareth. After supper we sat near the fire. John put wood in the fire and rearranged the embers to create toasty warmth as we sat and talked. Zebedee began his recollection of their encounter with the man I had come so far to see—twice. "David, you were right. This man who visited us a short while back is certainly the most fascinating person I've ever met. Your Jesus born in Bethlehem is a remarkable person. He has a wonderful way with words and a delightful sense of humor. He made us feel as if fishing were the most significant occupation in the world. I've never met a conversationalist with his skills."

John broke in at this point, "He discussed fishing in great detail. We asked him if he'd ever fished and the answer was that he had not but that he was interested in how fish are caught and boats and nets cared for. It was easy to talk to him because he was sincere and kind."

"That was how it was with me when we discussed my occupation," I commented. "He certainly gave the impression that he was truly interested in what shepherds do. I have never had another rabbi who looked upon shepherding with interest. In fact when I used to attend synagogue my rabbi was scornful of shepherds."

"Well, fishing is considered honorable only among fishermen, I think," James offered. "After all, there is an aroma associated with our profession which does not always make us the best of company." He smiled as he said these words. I smiled too. Shepherds can certainly be associated with unpleasant smells on occasion and I had handled some stinking sheep and lambs.

"Can you remember what he said ... what he asked? Can you remember his words? Will he come here again? Do you know if he went back to Nazareth? Has he started some sort of ministry? Was anyone with him? Did he mention his cousin John?" I was on a roll.

"Hold on! David, hold on!" Zebedee was laughing as he said this. "How can we answer you when you ask a dozen questions at once? You've probably just asked more questions than the number of fish we caught today." He was laughing, so the bad fishing day was no longer a tender topic.

Zebedee spoke first. "This man Jesus is a presence that is overpowering. We were all rapt each time he spoke. His interest in us was obvious. He was not thinking about himself during our time with him but only about us. Although we were hesitant to speak because of his aura, he made it easy for us to talk with him. His interest in fishing gave the impression that he wanted to become a fisherman and yet his demeanor indicated that he had much more significant things in mind for himself."

James added, "Jesus would look you in the eye and you felt as if he were searching your very soul. You wanted to drop your eyes and yet you didn't. You simultaneously wanted to hold his gaze as if you were unable to look away. It is hard to describe the feelings I had while he was with us."

There was a long silence. I had no desire to break it. These men had obviously experienced Jesus in the same way that I had. I wondered if they later tried to rethink his words and memorize everything they could remember.

These thoughts were broken by that very concept. John answered my mental questions. "We spent the rest of the day after he had gone trying to combine our memories and rethink every word he had spoken. You were right, David, this is no ordinary man. I, too, am obsessed with what he will do next. I heard his cousin speak. He was captivating but Jesus was ... I don't know ... hypnotic. He was also spellbinding, but in a different way. John made me want to repent. Jesus makes me want to ... to—" John stopped. "I don't know, David. He makes me want to do something but I can't put my finger on it. That sounds rather strange, I know, but I have been very restless and unfulfilled since his visit. I would like to go with you on this trip to Nazareth but today wasn't our first bad day and we need to keep fishing. I am eager to see you on your return from visiting him in Nazareth. I certainly see why you came back."

"I hope I didn't wait too long," I said. "I don't want to miss out when his 'time has come.' Did he indicate that he was returning to Nazareth?"

John was thinking intensely. I knew what he was doing because I'd been doing the same thing ever since meeting the man Jesus. John was reciting in his mind the words of the man. It seems as if everything he says, even in humor, is something you want to remember—not just a thought, but his exact words. John finally said, "Jesus said that he was going to Nazareth but that he had many things he needed to do and so little time for doing them." John paused. "From that I'd gather he was indicating that his 'time had come,' wouldn't you?"

I felt like turning and running towards Nazareth. I was so afraid I would miss something. My eagerness to get to Nazareth kept me awake long into the night—my imagination rambling through imaginary scenarios with Jesus. In the morning after we ate I gathered my belongings and promised the men that I would return and let them know what Jesus was doing. One thing I was sure of—all of us felt the same way about this charismatic man. I had the advantage of knowing first hand of the miraculous events surrounding his birth. These men felt the same way about Jesus without having seen angels announce him as the promised Messiah. They felt that way because of his presence, what he said, how he talked, and his deep personal interest in them.

18

Jesus Moves to Capernaum

This time I knew where I was going and had begun to feel comfortable among Galileans. After spending a lifetime in the shadows of Jerusalem and The Temple with the High Priest exerting influence over all religious leaders, I felt a burden lifted off my shoulders when I was in Galilee. You cannot say anything against the Jewish faith in many areas of Judea. Galilee did not have that sense of priestly 'presence' one felt in Bethlehem and its environs. Where I lived the priests seemed to be spying on us—even lowly shepherds. Of course, we were also at the mercy of our Roman oppressors. The tax collectors were those approved by Caesar and our tetrarch, Archelaus. The priests and Jewish leaders turned a blind eye as these Jewish tax collectors overcharged the citizens and pocketed the difference. There was little one could do when these crooks had the power of Judaism and Rome backing their excessive taxations.

I arrived in Nazareth late in the afternoon. I was hot and tired because I had rushed. I did not want to be on the road when night fell. I went to the well to refill my waterskin and there found one of Jesus' sisters. She spoke to me because she considered me a friend of the family. She told me she was married now and that only her mother and Jesus still lived at home. I asked how they were. "Jesus has made plans to begin to travel," she replied. "Mother will go with him."

"They are still at home now? You said they 'plan to travel?'" I was overly eager, but Elizabeth didn't seem to notice that.

"Yes, Jesus has a mission in life, he says, and he has been saving from his work at Sepphoris to finance his trip. Mother has never shown favoritism but I have always known that Jesus is somehow special. You have met him and talked with him. Don't you agree?"

I didn't need to think to answer that question. "Oh yes, he is a spellbinding person. In fact, that is why I have returned. I want to visit with him again."

Elizabeth smiled, "Well, it's a good thing you came when you did, because next week he will be away from Nazareth. He talks of his travels but I'm not sure where they'll take him. He's visited two towns by the Lake of Galilee and gotten to know some people there. Most of them are fishermen. He talked about two young men and their father—I remember his name—Zebedee—and also of some fishermen he met in Capernaum. I think from some of the things he said that he plans to go to Capernaum first." She stopped talking. "Why am I telling you all of these speculations of mine? You can go to the house and talk with Mother and Jesus yourself."

As she finished filling her water jars and skins I noticed that she was probably going to have a baby within three months. In my previous visit I had not thought about the other family members of the household or those married and gone. I had, of course, thought of Mary but my attitudes had changed. Perhaps when I visited with Mary and Jesus I should inquire of the other members of the family. I was still very self-conscious about being with this special family ... probably more so with no one else in the home except the two people whose interjection into my life had changed it forever. In spite of customs I insisted on carrying the heaviest of the water jugs for this pregnant woman. We passed Jesus' house on the way to Elizabeth's. I noticed that this young pregnant woman carried her water with grace whereas I was sweating and straining. She thanked me profusely as I waved goodbye to return to the house of her mother and brother only a short walk back.

As I approached the house of these exceptional people I relived the experience so many years ago of approaching my own home where this mother rested with her marvelous baby. So many things had changed and yet one thing had not changed. I walked towards the modest home with awe and humility. I was going into the presence of the Messiah, the Promised One who would bring peace to people. As convinced as I was many years ago that this person was very special to be announced to shepherds rather than priests and rabbis, I was even more convinced now that I was approaching the Messiah—wanting to be a part of his plans for Israel; actually his plans might be for more than Israel—after all, the magi had come from the Orient to participate in his wondrous birth.

When I reached the house I could see the lamp was lit and could hear the voices of Jesus and Mary as they talked. Not wanting to eavesdrop I quickly spoke up to announce my presence. "Hello, this is David of Bethlehem. I have come back as I promised two years ago."

"Please come in." This was spoken by the beautiful Mary whose voice sounded exactly as it had so many years earlier. I entered and had to resist the inclination to kneel before this holy man. After my studies of the scriptures, I was in awe of him. Immediately Jesus reminded me of his humanity. He laughed when I entered.

"David, it is so good to see you again. I recall telling you that I wanted to see you again when my time was right. You are intuitive because you came at exactly the right time. Please join us for a meal." His dark eyes searched my face and scanned my appearance. I was tired and sweaty from my rather hurried trip from Tiberias. I hadn't shaved since leaving Bethlehem and had a scruffy beard. As always, I carried my shepherd's crook and my slingshot was tucked in my waist-band.

Mary got a cloth, wet it and knelt at my feet to wash them as any proper host does after a guest's long journey. I could feel my face flush with embarrassment at this gesture. However, there was nothing to do but to accept this act of hospital-ity so I sat—but felt hot tears come to my eyes. This woman kneeling at my feet had given birth to the Son of God. I shrugged my shoulders up hoping to wipe away the tears unnoticed. Jesus turned to get the meal which was ready to be eaten. I think he saw my humility and shame and was allowing me privacy.

I was eager to learn of Jesus' plans and to find out if I could be a part of his ministry. However, I didn't want to appear brash so I waited to see what devel-oped since Jesus had already indicated that he would fill me in on what was hap-pening. Jesus began to talk and I just listened. "David, I told you that I had a mission in life and that it was not building Roman structures at Sepphoris. Now that my youngest sister is married I am no longer needed here as the father figure. I have plans to begin traveling and teaching Israel what they have forgotten and abandoned. My father—and by this I mean Yahweh—is very disappointed in the direction His people have taken. He has sent prophets and given Israel the Torah, teachings, history, prophets—Jewish leaders have in their hands what my father wants from them. Yet they are not obeying the teachings of the scriptures and they are leading his people in completely the wrong direction. My father's efforts to reach his people are ineffective and he has sent me as a personal emissary to lead the people back to him. My mother wants to go with me. We plan to leave in two days. My brother James will live in this house as he has more children than his small house can accommodate. We are preparing for our work and will be glad for you to join us."

I was ecstatic … and scared. What can a shepherd do for such a person or for such a mission? I was totally inadequate for whatever he had planned. However, I wouldn't want to miss this opportunity to be with Jesus and hear him teach and tell his jokes and stories. He patiently waited as I processed these thoughts. "Yes,

I am already prepared to travel, of course, and would appreciate the opportunity to accompany you on this journey."

"Actually, we aren't traveling far at this time. My mother and I will be going to Capernaum. We have come to know some fishermen from there and my plans include some of these fishermen. I am a Galilean and my mission will begin in Galilee. I have taught here in Nazareth but it is difficult to get people who have known you all your life to consider you as an emissary from God. To the people of this town I am Jesus, son of Joseph. Perhaps later in my ministry my friends here will recognize me as the Messiah, but not at this time."

This reminded me of the night the angels appeared to a group of shepherds and the rabbi ridiculed us for making such a claim. I understood Jesus' rejection at Nazareth because I had experienced the same thing. I wondered if these people would believe if they saw angels who assured them that Jesus was the Son of God. When Jesus spoke again it was eerie because it was as if he had read my mind. "David, some people won't believe no matter what is said or what revelations they have. You had a revelation and you believe."

"But," I offered, "when I was here two years ago I heard you talk. It was obvious you were special. Don't the people who know you well see what I saw in a short visit?"

"David, you still had the advantage of *knowing* in advance that I was the one announced by angels. You will meet arrogant people, cynical people, gullible people and sincere, honest seekers. My mission is to reach all of these types of people—even if they have never seen angels or other miracles."

Again I recognized the wisdom of this man Jesus. Yes, I had a decided advantage over most people. Only two other shepherds from that miraculous night were still living and both were old and feeble—one, of course, being my uncle Nathan. I was the only shepherd who had experienced the angels able to be here in Nazareth with the man the baby had become. Yet we were sharing a meal in his humble home. I couldn't grasp the "Son of God" concept but I accepted it because of the vision of the angels. Across from me, wearing the beautiful coat made by my mother, was the Messiah.

Mary broke into my thoughts, "David, please plan to sleep by the fire. You've had a long journey and I'm sure are tired. Tomorrow will be a big day for all of us."

In spite of my excitement I had no trouble sleeping. I had rushed to arrive in Nazareth before dark and was very tired. Besides that—there was something soothing about Jesus' presence. Of course it helped also that I saw Mary as the mother of Jesus. She was still a stunningly beautiful woman in my eyes but I had completely overcome my enchantment with her. I dreamed about Jesus, Mary and fishermen on the Lake of Galilee.

In the morning we all busied ourselves preparing the house for its new occupants and gathering what we needed for our journey in which Jesus and Mary would move to a different town. They had arranged to borrow a burro from a friend who would be in Capernaum later in the week and would pick up his animal while there.

We departed after a light midday meal and led the animal down out of the hills to the lakeshore. The journey to Tiberias was some fifteen miles so we would have to stay the night in that town on the western shore of Lake Galilee. The journey to Capernaum was another ten miles or so following the shoreline north. I recommended Josiah's fish fry and his wife Anna's bread for our evening meal. Of course I was hoping to find Zebedee and his sons there. I told Jesus about these fishermen who were so impressed with him and wanted me to report back to them concerning my visit to Nazareth. Jesus laughed and promised to report to them in person. Josiah outdid himself with the meal he prepared for the three of us. It was a feast eaten in his home with his family. Josiah and Anna were overjoyed to share their home with Jesus and his mother. His sons gave up their pallets for the three travelers and we were treated as honored guests. After we had eaten supper Jesus began his storytelling. Again I was stunned at his ability to hold his audience. His stories were about everyday things and yet each anecdote was told with such finesse that his audience—including his mother and me—was spellbound. When Jesus reminded us that it was quite late we were all disappointed that the stories would end and amazed at how long we had listened while he talked.

I again tried to memorize everything that he had said. This time I realized I could not do that and so began to create in my mind a list of the stories he had told. I repeated the mental list several times and then began to analyze the first of these accounts. I knew from previous experience that everything he said had deeper meanings that would reveal themselves if I pondered them long enough. I managed to delve into two such stories before I found myself being awakened by stirring in Josiah's house.

After I had washed and shaved, I found that Anna had been up for at least two hours as there was fresh leavened bread baking in the oven and Josiah was out preparing fish to go with the bread and goat cheese. His sons were gathering firewood and his two daughters were preparing for the men to have breakfast together. I greeted the ladies and joined the men as we lay down to eat while the bread and fish were fresh and warm. We could hear the girls giggling in the adjacent room as they ate and talked about how handsome John, son of Zebedee was. I smiled as I overheard that because I had been struck by young John's eyes and wondered if girls found them irresistible. Apparently they did indeed!

19

John Baptizes Jesus

During the morning meal Josiah told us that Jesus' cousin John was angering Herod Antipas. Jesus decided to go to where the young man was preaching in the wilderness. We left with a sense of urgency that I did not understand. John had been preaching for a rather long period of time but Jesus seemed eager to get there as quickly as possible. We were an unusual trio, a tall man with a Judean accent carrying the crook of a shepherd, another also tall slender man with the rugged sinew of a working person, with both of the men wearing very fine woven woolen robes. With us was a beautiful woman with wisps of gray in her long dark hair and her dark eyes regularly falling lovingly on the handsome man in the seamless coat who was obviously her son. To my surprise Jesus didn't talk much even though we walked together for almost four hours. The sky was heavily over-cast with dark low clouds creating a sense of gloom. When we saw the crowds I spoke up saying, unnecessarily, "John will be nearby. He always draws crowds like this." Most of the people, again, were peasants and there was even a scatter-ing of people who were gentiles, by their dress. A number of Roman soldiers were there, in uniform. I assumed they were there to control the crowd until I noticed among the group approaching the Jordan three soldiers who had removed all of their metal in preparation for the baptism of repentance. Jesus walked through the crowds with his long legs. I could maintain his pace and his weaving through the throngs of people, but Mary was having difficulty keeping up with us so I stayed with her and helped propel us both forward towards the evangelist. John was approaching the Jordan with a following of penitents and was not preaching. Jesus turned to his mother and removed his beautiful coat, folded it and laid it across his mother's arms. He then walked forward, joining the group moving toward the river for John's baptism. When John stepped into the Jordan he turned to face the people and caught sight of his cousin Jesus walking straight towards him. John, who had seemed all confidence on each occasion prior to this, appeared to be dumbfounded. His face froze and his body didn't even twitch as he watched his cousin continue to walk boldly towards him. Even the line of people awaiting baptism seemed frozen in place as the dark haired young man approached John.

In the gloom of the lowering skies Jesus said simply, "I want to be baptized."

John was aghast. "Master, you do not need baptism. Please baptize me."

"John," Jesus said, "this is what God wants me to do. God wants you to baptize me. My mission is at hand."

The man with the long hair and beard; wearing goatskins and leather sandals tied with sinew to his weathered feet, bowed his head. Then, with tears in his eyes, John gently and lovingly lowered his cousin into the Jordan. Mary and I had reached the edge of the crowd at this point and I saw Jesus' mother begin to cry also. I realized that I had my arm around the woman I had once dreamed about. I blushed as I removed it slowly. As I watched Jesus, rising from the waters of his baptism, a slit opened in the black cloud and brilliant sunlight broke through the small hole in the cloud. The beam of sunlight fell on Jesus—no one else—just Jesus. In this huge crowd there was silence. John had stepped away from his cousin but the sunbeam was so isolated it would not have illuminated the baptizer if he'd been right beside Jesus. It reminded me of the night of the angels and the bright light. Then I saw another unusual phenomenon and knew that it *was* like the night of the angels. I knew these visions were acts of God, whom Jesus had called Father. A dove, the bird of peace, flew down—never veering out of that narrow beam of sunlight—and lit on the shoulder of the Prince of Peace. I heard a voice coming from above saying, "This is my beloved son in whom I am well pleased." (Matthew 3) I looked at Mary to see if she had seen and heard what I had seen and heard but her tears would have blurred whatever she saw. As Jesus stepped out of the water, the opening in the cloud closed. I knew that I had again experienced God himself and had not the slightest doubt that I was traveling with the Son of God. Although I was unaware of the reaction of the crowd to this miracle, I recall that in that very large throng of people—some of whom were children—there was silence while these things took place. Mary and I followed her son as we walked silently through the crowd of people who now parted as the Red Sea must have parted for Moses. I could hear John speaking into the silence, "This is the one I have been telling you about. This is the Messiah. You have today seen the Son of God. I am not worthy to tie his shoes yet I have baptized him."

20

Jesus Goes into the Wilderness

We had walked until we were away from everyone. Jesus broke our silence. He looked into my eyes and said, "David, I need some time alone. Please take my mother to Capernaum where we have arranged a place to live. Mother, I need to spend time with my father. My time is come and I must determine his will. Do not worry about me; I will come to you when I am finished here." He kissed her gently on the forehead and turned towards the wilderness. We stood together without speaking—watching as he faded from sight.

Mary was the one who finally spoke. "He is so intense. I knew when the angel told me I would have this special child that as his mother I would experience many things not normal to motherhood. I didn't realize how much I would worry about him. Isn't that silly?! I worry about the Son of God. But he is *my* son and worry goes with being a mother. He hasn't told me what to expect now that 'his time has come' but I know that he speaks out against the religious leaders and that does not bode well for anyone in Israel. John has angered Herod Antipas and I have heard that Antipas is trying to find a way to bring an end to the preaching of John." We were walking slowly now. I was tired and I knew she would be much more tired and emotionally exhausted after watching her special son walk away into a wilderness area to spend time with God. Fortunately we had left our belongings at Josiah's house and so were unencumbered. In fact, I began to smell the fish frying as these thoughts were going through my mind. We could not go to Capernaum today because it was too late and we were both tired. When we neared Josiah the jovial man called out to us to come and eat.

Even jolly Josiah sensed the emotional depth of the moment. Both Mary and I were pensive and inattentive to our surroundings. I was remembering what had happened at the Jordan River. I suppose Mary was also, but she had much more on her mind because she was concerned about her son's venture into the wilderness. The area into which he had been headed as he left us was arid and inhospitable. He would find little water there and certainly no food. Jesus' only company would most likely be wild animals. I was wishing I could have gone with him, having experience with the dangers of a wilderness area. We ate with almost no conversation and Mary went to her bed. I went out to the pier and sat watching the moon over the lake. I mentally retraced the scriptures I had studied with the Essenes. I recalled a very old story from my childhood: Noah had released a dove from the ark to determine if the waters had receded. The dove did not return and Noah recognized that the storm and its aftermath were over. I thought about this and tried to decipher the meaning of the dove. A dove symbolizes peace. Perhaps this was a reminder that Jesus is the Prince of Peace. I wondered if the storm were about to begin. Jesus said it was time. Mary said he riled our religious leaders. How I hate them! All we could do was to wait. I finally went into the house, which was quiet but for Josiah's gentle snores, and walked quietly to my pallet to enter a restless sleep.

In the morning our spirits were lifted by Josiah's singing and his laughter. We ate and told the family of the experience with John the baptizer. Jesus had told his mother and me to continue to Capernaum and so we set out in the morning for the northernmost city on the lake. Our trip took us through the small town of Magdala where we stopped and ate the lunch sent with us by Josiah and Anna. This was the town where Zebedee lived. We had actually passed his home between Tiberias and Capernaum where I had once been a guest. When we were passing, I checked the house but no one was home and we continued our journey. Capernaum was a bustling metropolis. Mary and I walked an extra mile before she recognized the house Jesus had arranged to be their home for a time. Although I insisted that I could stay outside without any discomfort, Mary assured me that the roof had a sleeping area where I could stay for as long as needed until Jesus returned. She insisted that I stay there because she was more comfortable in a strange city with a friend within calling distance. So I arranged my belongings on the roof with the understanding that I would sleep by the hearth in the main room if the weather became unfavorable. We cared for the burro and took him to the local stable where the owner would pick him up.

Jesus had left his mother with a supply of money for her needs while he was away. The house was paid for in advance and so the two of us shared expenses as we purchased needed supplies. It hadn't really been discussed but I was staying in order to be there and see what the Son of God would do when his time came. Mary had openly expressed her need for the security of a trusted man in the house. I also had not yet mentioned my friend in Jericho, Bart, who wanted the Messiah to heal his blindness.

After two weeks had passed Mary and I began to become greatly concerned about her son. He had gone into a desolate area. However, he had assured her that he would return when he had done what needed to be done there. We both reminded ourselves that the baptism had been a further reminder that Yahweh was indeed aware of his son and what he was doing. Jesus had said this trip was his father's will and so we continued to wait.

While familiarizing ourselves with the city of Capernaum, I used the pier as my retreat and often went there to look across the lake. I recognized Zebedee's boat and would try to see if their fishing was good. However, this northern part of the lake was taken by other fishing boats. One of these boats docked one day while I was on the pier. The men reminded me of James and John in that they were two brothers who seemed to work well together. One of the brothers, Simon, was tall, muscular and brash. His brother Andrew was shy and soft spoken. When they came in Simon called out to me asking for my help. He threw me the line and as I held it the two young men alit. The large one, Simon, tied the boat to the pier. Two older men, hired servants, assisted the owner brothers in unloading the day's catch. After seeing Zebedee's successes and failures, I recognized this as a rather poor fishing day. However, the men seemed in good spirits and Simon paid the two workers in fish, stating that because there weren't enough fish to sell, this was their day's wages. This was, of course, when I realized that the two young men were the owners and the older men hirelings. Andrew asked me to select fish as payment for my help with the ropes. I knew the kind of fish Mary had selected at Josiah's and so chose one of those. Andrew gave me another, for my wife, he said.

"I'm not married. Perhaps you have me confused with someone else," I said.

"Sir," Andrew flushed as he spoke. "I saw you earlier today on this pier with a beautiful dark haired lady. I assumed she was your wife. You may still keep the fish," he added softly.

"I—I am a friend of the family." My mind immediately shook me with the realization that these men who would be seeing us regularly might think of Mary as living with a man who is not her husband. "Mary's son, a rabbi named Jesus had to be away for a while. He asked me to care for his mother." I mentally raced back through these words as the men looked at me curiously.

"You're no Galilean," the big man said.

"No," I stammered. "No, but Jesus was born during the census proscribed by Herod the Great. She—his mother—and her husband had to go from Nazareth to Bethlehem for that. They stayed with my parents after the baby was born and so we came to know them." Again my brain was telling me I was still off track.

These men were younger than Jesus and probably never heard of the census. "Actually, I am the lady's guest and will be going to her house from here. She will receive the fish with your compliments." I hesitated. "I sleep on the roof. Come with me and I'll show you. Her son is away and I am assisting her as she settles in Capernaum." I wasn't sure what to tell and what to withhold. I certainly didn't want to embarrass Mary but also didn't want these men thinking her immoral. I babbled on, trying to remove such assumptions. "Mary has a son who is very special. They are moving here from Nazareth but her son is meeting another obligation and will be coming later. I am a friend of the family. My name is David. I am a shepherd from Bethlehem. Well, I was a shepherd." I was not making things better. "I came from Nazareth with Mary, the lady, and her son Jesus. We went to the Jordan River south of the Lake of Galilee and heard John the baptizer preach. Jesus asked John, who is his cousin, to baptize him." This was ridiculous! I'm sure I sounded like an idiot. "I'm sorry. There is a long story. Perhaps I can tell you another time. Thank you for the fish." I turned away. Simon was laughing heartily at my incoherence. I walked away hearing the raucous laughter of Simon the fisherman and his brother quietly trying to get him to stop embarrassing me.

I learned that these fishermen needed help unloading their boat after a good day of fishing. So I began to watch the lake and determine if I could make myself available when the boats came in. I offered to do this without pay, but the brothers always insisted on giving me fish, and some of the fishermen insisted on paying me. Perhaps this was not a bad idea because my funds would not last forever and it was obvious that Jesus was not returning as quickly as his mother and I had anticipated.

21

Jesus Returns from the Wilderness

One day I was walking along the shore and watching the boats when I saw an emaciated figure walking towards me wearing the coat my mother had made. I don't think I would have recognized him if he had not been wearing the coat. He was clean but his appearance was pathetic. I ran to meet him, afraid he would not even be able to walk the rest of the way to the house. I offered him my arm and could feel his bones as we walked slowly towards the house where his mother was. I waited for him to talk. He said nothing except a few words of gratitude for the help. As we neared the house his mother saw us coming. She ran to the door and began sobbing as she kissed her son on his hands, his face, his sunken chest. I didn't want to intrude on such a personal reunion and so as soon as Jesus was seated I excused myself as Mary rushed to get nourishment for her obviously famished son.

I went to the pier and watched the overcast sky. Rain would be welcome but I was glad Jesus was safely in his house because I was not sure his body could take any setbacks. He had been gone over a month and looked as if he'd not eaten the entire time. I sat there pondering his appearance. When the rain began I remained on the pier. Most of the fishermen continued fishing as if nothing was different. They were not catching many fish, however, and so I didn't see myself with a job unloading when the boats came in. After an hour I walked to the baker's house and purchased bread. We already had fish and dried meat. I went to the marketplace and bought figs, dates, nuts, olives and oil. It had stopped raining and I returned to the house laden down with food for the three of us and obsessed with questions I dared not ask about where the Messiah had been for those many weeks.

"David!" Jesus spoke with a tone of authority. He had my full attention. "I appreciate what you did for my mother while I was gone. I'm sorry to have left you with a burden. I did what I had to do."

"Teacher," I began, "it was no burden. Your mother is a gracious lady and her company is always a pleasure. Sir, can I get anything for you?" I stood still—my arms still full of the provisions I had just bought.

"David, I think you have already gotten more than I can eat in a week's time. Let's have lunch."

I realized I was still holding the food I had bought and began to display it on the table near the hearth. I wanted to help him down to the mat for his meal but hesitated and Mary's quick head movement stopped me. We sat and Mary placed the food before us and joined us. I noticed blisters on his feet. His skin was drawn and darkened by many, many hours in the sun. Beyond his appearance there was something else about him that was different. I watched him, trying to determine the aura I sensed. He didn't speak. We ate in silence. I certainly wasn't going to be the person who broke that silence. I felt like an outsider intruding on an extremely intimate occasion.

Mary finally spoke. We had finished eating, and she asked us if we would like some wine. I waited for Jesus to reply. "Yes, Mother, please bring some of the wine David bought. We need to drink a wine of fellowship and mission." He took the bread I had brought and broke off three pieces, passing one to Mary and the other to me. He poured wine into three cups and passed these. "Let us eat and drink to our mission," he said. Before we ate he led us in a prayer of dedication to his father's mission. The servings were small and this was appropriate because of the effect wine has on me. After we had the bread and wine I went to my sleeping quarters on the roof. My mat and cloak were in the house during the rain and sleeping was easy that night because of the cooling from the rain and because the rabbi had returned. I went to sleep wondering where I would be living now that the man of the house was home.

In the morning I waited to allow Jesus and his mother time together. I was very close to my mother and felt I understood the relationship. However, theirs was certainly different from mine in that Mary knew her son was the Son of God and that he had a mission. Whether she understood that mission or not I could not know. I certainly didn't. Jesus came up onto the roof and asked me to come down and join them for a morning meal. I washed and shaved before eating.

Jesus looked better even after such a short time back. When he'd arrived his eyes were sunken and even through the sunburn his skin looked sallow. Now his eyes were lively and his smile was back. "David, I can never thank you enough for caring for my mother during these many weeks. I shall be busy from now on and may need your help caring for her from time to time. I have given her permission to tell you some of the things that are happening because you are family to me. However, I do not wish to keep you from your own plans."

I waited for him to continue. When he did not, after a pause I replied, "Teacher, I left the sheep with my relatives. Both of my parents have died. I have no siblings and have never married. I have come to Nazareth twice to see you because of what happened in Bethlehem many years ago. I have studied the scriptures. I know you are the Promised One. I know that you are the Messiah. From what you have said, I know that you are not here to overthrow the Romans. I am not sure what your 'mission' is, but I feel I must be a part of it—but only with your permission. I will do as you tell me. I have a friend in Jericho who has asked me to bring the Messiah to him because he was born blind. He wants you to heal him. I am confused about my role in all of this that involves you, but I think I have a role. Please tell me what it is that you want from me." I knew that I had just said a lot and expected him to need time to think about it.

"David, you do have a role in my mission. However, I need young men for my core group of followers because they will have many years in which to complete the mission that I begin. Right now your role is with me and with my mother. Please stay as our guest as I begin my work."

I was thrilled! And scared! And filled with awe! And ... and ... full of questions that I dared not ask. So I thanked the teacher and dropped my gaze from his eyes. His look was one of patience and understanding. I felt as if he could read my very soul. I felt my face flush and I tried to cover this by putting the cup of water to my mouth.

Jesus asked to be excused and left while his mother and I sat by the fire. She began to tell me about his experience in the wilderness. Of course she began by requesting confidence because no one else knew of these events. Because I was already a believer—actually for more than thirty years I had been, I suppose—and because I had maintained that confidence, both mother and son knew I could be trusted. Mary told me about the temptations Jesus had recounted from his wilderness experience and about the fasting he had endured. It was no wonder he looked so emaciated upon his return—I couldn't even see how he could make the journey. He had eaten in Tiberias but had continued home non-stop. Mary told me that he had spent the forty days with God—and with temptation—because he needed to understand temptation in order to be fully human. And he needed the time with God in order to plan his mission. After she finished I asked no questions. Mary told me that she had an enormous storehouse of memories of this particular son. She rejoiced to be able to share them with me.

Mary asked for my permission to repeat some of the many stories because she needed this opportunity to refresh these memories.

She then told me a story from Jesus' childhood. When he was twelve years old many citizens of Nazareth had traveled together to Jerusalem for Passover. Jesus had been with some of the other families during the trip from Nazareth but Joseph and Mary had joined him when they were in Jerusalem and the family was together for the Passover celebration. Mary and Joseph had left their other children with neighbors but Jesus was old enough to be a part of this most significant of Jewish celebrations: the saving of Jews from slavery. On the return journey Jesus had started out with the same friends. Mary and Joseph assumed their son was sharing the tent with his friends but could not find him on the second day along the road. As they frantically sent word throughout the caravan it became obvious that he was not anywhere to be found. The parents had rushed back to Jerusalem and finally were told that there was a little boy in the Temple. They prayed earnestly as they made their way to the Temple where they had found the child. Jesus had been a good student in synagogue but when they found him he was with the leaders of the Temple, not just their local rabbi. And, when they'd entered the room they heard the high pitched voice of a boy expounding on the prophets. The voice they heard was that of their son. The Pharisees, Sadducees, priests, rabbis—these leaders were the listeners. No one else was speaking—only the twelve-year old boy. Their reaction as parents was to reveal their anguish from these frightening days of rushing about looking for him and fearing that they might never find him. Jesus had looked into his mother's eyes and told her with a serenity she did not feel, "Why did you worry about me? I needed to be here, in my father's house." I shared with Mary that this story had reached Bethlehem but when I'd heard it no one knew anything else about the incident. I told her that I had realized by the boy's age that this could be the same Jesus who spent his first two weeks of life in our home.

We were both emotionally drained and needed time to think. I helped with clearing away the dishes, in spite of her insistence that this was a woman's job. I then went on a walk along the shore and to the boat dock. I seemed able to think best watching that calm lake. The sky was deep blue but filled with large white clouds. I lay on my back on the pier and spent a long time considering all that had taken place in the short time since the return of Mary's son. I wondered what was next.

We did not have to wait very long. Word reached Capernaum that John the Baptist had been arrested by Herod Antipas. I had known that John was openly criticizing Herod for marrying his brother's wife and anticipated something like this, but it was frightening, nonetheless. The arrest had taken place while Jesus was in the wilderness but we only learned of it after his return to Capernaum.

When I reached the house to tell Mary of John's arrest, Jesus was there and I told them both. Jesus looked profoundly saddened. He said something strange. He said, "John has done his job. Now it is time for me to do mine." Mary and I looked at each other—our faces filled with questions—as Jesus then walked from the house. For the first time I wrapped both of my arms around the woman who had once been the love of my heart. I did so unselfconsciously. It was a brotherly action and we both recognized it as such. When Mary stood back away from me I could feel the dampness on my shoulder which I knew were her tears. I then went out to see where Jesus was going with such determination. He went to the center of town and began to speak to whoever would listen, "Where are your riches?" he asked his listeners. "If you store up riches on earth they will not last. You must store your riches in heaven. How do you store riches in heaven? By obeying God my father. The kingdom of heaven is the only worthy goal in life. Riches become the goal in life of many people. And many people become rich because their hearts are dedicated to wealth." He continued, telling a story of a starving man who begged at the gate of the house of a rich man, who would throw the poor starving man food as he would to dogs. He concluded this story with a reference to heaven in which the starving beggar is in heaven and the rich man in hell. There is no question this would offend the religious aristocracy, especially the Sadducees who did not believe in an afterlife. He gave several memorable illustrations of the value of the kingdom of God—using lost coins and, to my delight—lost sheep as illustrations.

In my studies of the scriptures, I'd not encountered this terminology. I wanted to ask my teacher, "What is the 'Kingdom of God?" But for the time being I wanted to listen to the rabbi. A small crowd began to gather. One of the fishing boats came in, with almost no fish, and the big man Simon disembarked, helped his brother off the boat and after tying up the boat they joined the small crowd listening to Jesus. Someone in the group asked Jesus if he had heard of the arrest of the prophet John. Jesus assured him that John could be silenced but that his message could never be stopped. Jesus stated that John's message of repentance was for everyone because everyone had sinned. He then asked for his hearers to repent. Not everyone stayed to listen. One rabbi asked him where he got the authority to speak for God. Jesus didn't even reply to him. Jesus locked eyes with the teacher and stared at him without speaking. The other rabbi dropped his head and turned and walked away. I don't think it was in anger; I think he just didn't know what to say next. Those in the audience wearing phylacteries and the accoutrements of devout followers of "The Law" were the ones walking away. After a while Jesus thanked his remaining audience and returned to his home. He went onto the roof and I knew to give him privacy. I went back into the market-place to listen to conversations about the new prophet of Capernaum.

Jesus continued with this teaching in public places in Capernaum for two weeks and then announced to his mother that he needed to return to Nazareth. He asked me to stay in Capernaum and wait for his return. I agreed to keep things in order in his house and give him this time with his family.

22

Jesus and Mary Return from Nazareth Visit

They returned two weeks later. Mary told me about the trip back home. Jesus had gone into the marketplace in Nazareth to preach his message of repentance and the good news of the coming of the Kingdom of God. Although he had previously been a popular raconteur and loved by children, he was not accepted as a prophet. When he went into his hometown to preach repentance, his friends saw a different man and began to jeer at him because they only saw him as a carpenter and story-teller. Children would come when he would begin to preach, but without the stories and without the humor, his demands for repentance were repugnant to those who had known him all of his life. He returned to Capernaum dejected but still determined to fulfill his mission.

On his third day back he was walking by the lake. It was late on a Friday afternoon. Simon and his brother Andrew were mending nets at the dock. Jesus called out to them, "Follow me and I will teach you how to fish for people." I was sitting on the pier and saw the two men immediately lay down the nets, get out of the boat and just walk away with Jesus. What a strange sensation! I had, I suppose, done something similar, but I was not young. These men surely had families to support and couldn't just walk away from their livelihoods. However, it appeared that is just what they did. I joined the threesome, listening as Jesus talked about fishing and about his mission. When we came to the next boat dock Zebedee and his sons and hired hands were in the boat and were also mending the nets. Jesus looked up and called the two young men, James and John by name. "Follow me!" was all he said to them. They laid down the nets and told their father goodby and joined the three of us. I was not fully a part of this group because Jesus was asking them questions about fishing and discussing his mission. These men had frequently been in the audience when Jesus had been preaching a few weeks earlier. But to see them just walk away from their livelihoods—no questions asked, was astonishing. I don't think I could have done that except for the miracles I had seen: the angels at his birth and the voice from heaven at his baptism. These men had only heard Jesus' message and apparently dropped everything to follow him.

23

The Ministry Continues

As the sun settled behind the mountains everyone went home in order to honor the Sabbath. Although I had not been to synagogue since being jeered by the rabbi in Bethlehem, I learned that Jesus intended to be the rabbi in synagogue in the morning. Of course I wanted to attend. This was an experience that I thank God I did not miss. We entered the synagogue—a motley group of men. Mary went to the women's side while I joined the four fishermen and Jesus on the men's side. This was not like any of the boring synagogue experiences of my childhood! Before Jesus began to speak a crazy man entered the room shouting. I expected someone to apprehend him but he walked boldly forward to Jesus and shouted in his face. He demanded that Jesus leave; that he had come to destroy the synagogue at Capernaum. He shouted that he knew Jesus was the Son of God. This really caught my attention. As far as I knew this was not known by more than a handful of people, including myself. Jesus did not speak to the man but to the evil spirit in him which was actually doing the speaking. Jesus commanded the evil spirit to leave the man. The man fell to the floor, convulsing, and then went limp. He was drenched in sweat. When he recovered he was like an ordinary person. He spoke softly and apparently had no memories of his behavior a short time earlier. The priests were aghast. Can a good person be on speaking terms with evil spirits? Or was Jesus also an evil spirit? Most of those present were amazed at his authority and ability to perform a miracle. When the scriptures had been read and discussed the people left talking among themselves about what they had seen.

Jesus went home with his new follower Simon and his brother Andrew. The other fishermen accompanied them. I took Mary home. It was later that I learned from John about Jesus' second miracle on that amazing Sabbath. When the group of men arrived at Simon's home they found Simon's mother-in-law very ill with a high fever. Her face was flushed with the fever and she was in a coma. Jesus had entered the sick woman's room and asked for privacy. Simon, who had remained in the room, said Jesus knelt beside her bed, looked heavenward and took her hand. She arose immediately from the bed and began to prepare a meal for this group of fishermen and Jesus as if nothing had happened. When John was telling me about the incident, he insisted that he had seen the woman and that she was very ill and flushed with fever. He said she was healed the instant Jesus touched her. So when Jesus went out that evening after sundown, I did not want to miss a moment and stayed as close to him as I was able.

Crowds began to assemble near Jesus' house. He stepped back towards the pier and as people approached him he healed the sick of body and of mind. I was near the four fishermen and we all just watched in awe. Mary had gone to the roof of her house in order to see without being shoved about by the crowds of people. I saw her watching. She appeared frightened and yet proud of her son.

When it became dark and the crowds dissipated, I returned to the house. Jesus entered a short time later. He did not eat but went to the roof. Later, after I had eaten, I went to the pier and waited for him to descend into the house before taking my sleeping provisions to the roof. I lay awake for a long time remembering so much of what I had studied in Qumran with the Essenes. The Messiah had come and he really could heal the sick. I thought of my friend Bart in Jericho. I had mentioned him to Jesus. I prayed that Jesus' ministry would take him out of Galilee and into Jericho. Bartimaeus would learn the joy of sight. The Son of God would fulfill the prophecies. Indeed, the blind would see; the deaf would hear and the lame would walk. Jesus was the Messiah and he came to bring sight to the blind—of both soul and body. I praised God that I had lived to see this day and to know the Messiah.

In the morning, before dawn, I heard muffled footsteps. In the moonlight I could discern by his walk that Jesus was heading towards the hills. To my surprise, Simon had slept on the dock and he called the other fishermen who joined him in following Jesus out of town. This was that core group of 'young' men that the teacher had told me he needed for his mission. I watched them walk into the night. I later learned that the group had prayed for over an hour until the sun rose.

24

The Ministry Expands

At breakfast I was both surprised and honored when Jesus asked me to stay and help care for his mother. He needed to accelerate his ministry and he would return for us when he was ready.

So Mary and I began to receive the news. Jesus had chosen other men—all young—to join him in his ministry. There were twelve whom he called his Apostles. And each had been chosen in like manner as I had seen the four fishermen selected. Jesus would approach a person and say simply, "Follow me," and in most cases the man asked no questions but just left what he was doing and followed. There were some who made excuses—that they had family matters to attend to or that they needed to see to their estates. Jesus simply moved on and selected others. This group of twelve plus Jesus was itinerant and even went into gentile areas. Amazing stories of Jesus' miracles were circulating throughout Capernaum and reaching other areas of Israel. I don't know if the arrogant religious leaders of Jerusalem were getting reports on the miracles of Jesus or not, but doubted they would accept the stories. They certainly had not been included in the miraculous birth event. In fact, here in Capernaum the Pharisees were passing the word that it was all faked. The rabbis in synagogue were teaching that what we were hearing of Jesus' miracles were lies—that the sick were part of the act and those from whom demons were cast out had faked it. Sadducees, who rarely got along with Pharisees, were echoing the news that Jesus was deceiving his audience and Jews needed to avoid contact with the man. One of their strongest arguments was that Jesus was going into gentile territories and offering his "Kingdom of God" to non-Jews. They pointed out the absurdity of this. Jews were God's chosen people and anyone who opened the doors to God's Kingdom to non-Jews was obviously a heretic. The healing of Simon's mother-in-law was another prime example they used. Of course she would fake illness because Simon was one of the brainwashed followers of the self-proclaimed "Messiah." So Mary and I heard rumors and sometimes mourned at the horrible things being said about her son.

The twelve chosen apostles were openly jeered by the Jewish leadership. They reminded their hearers that Jesus had chosen a group of ignorant people of no social or religious standing for his so-called "leaders." The Pharisees were particularly scathing in their opinions of the ones Jesus was training for his ministry. "Fishermen!" they would shout; "Fishermen and a tax collector!" They would spit out these words with venom. "The Messiah is going to save Israel with a bunch of ignorant laborers!" I found these words painful and tried to protect Mary from hearing such rumors but I think she may have heard more than I did because women congregate at the well and converse at length.

So we waited and listened. There was no doubt that Jesus was making impressions. Sometimes people were healed and sometimes they were not. We even heard a rumor that he had healed the servant of a Roman centurion. The Jews were furious at this. *I* was furious at this! Here is a man claiming to be the Messiah—the Savior who is not saving Jews from Roman oppression but is actually reputedly performing his healing miracles on the very ones leading the oppression of Jews. Some of the older Jews remembered the slaughter of thousands of Jews at the hands of the Romans when Herod the Great died and his son Archelaus in Jerusalem avenged the rejoicing exhibited by Jewish leaders at the funeral. All of my experiences with Jesus in public were that he was unconcerned about whom he offended when he spoke. He talked of the false piety of many religious leaders and ridiculed their obsessions with the law while they showed no concern for their fellow man. Many of his illustrations used religious leaders in a disparaging way. Of course he knew as well as I did that openly criticizing and offending the Jewish leaders could not win support from them in his ministry. I had to assume that he was not interested in their support. In fact, I felt that he must have seen it necessary to show the general public that their leadership was not valid.

The day finally came when the men returned. Mary and I rejoiced to see her son again. I was especially happy to see my fishermen friends. Those four men were friends of mine before they became apostles and I snatched the opportunity to glean from them any information about all that we had been hearing during their weeks of absence. When I spoke to Simon he proudly corrected me, "My new name is Peter," he said. "The Master says I am like a rock. David, you should have seen the things we have seen! Jesus is amazing! And, David, when he speaks he talks to the people. He doesn't need scrolls—he recites passages from the prophets. He uses stories to teach. I have never heard someone who can hold an audience breathless as he does. I confess that some of his stories that seem simple become complicated when I lie awake meditating on them. And some of his stories have not yet made sense to me. This is my weakness, not his. If I think about them long enough I learn from them. Andrew and I discuss things and he often has insights that I have missed. So do some of the others. Sometimes we are all just confused. But, David, he heals. He doesn't expect us to know every nuance of the Law as do our rabbis. In fact, he has angered the Pharisees and Sadducees repeatedly by disregarding some of their meticulous interpretations of the Law."

"Simon," I began.

"Peter!" he proudly corrected me. "Peter—the Rock!"

"Peter," I tried again. "Peter, does he still talk about the Kingdom of God?"

"Oh yes, that is his primary theme."

"Peter, what *is* the Kingdom of God?" I asked.

"David, I'm not sure. I told you that we don't understand everything he says. He speaks in parables and mysterious phrases. The Kingdom of God is one of these phrases. He prays a lot. When we asked him how to pray he included the phrase 'Your kingdom come on earth as it is in heaven.' So—whatever God's Kingdom is, Jesus taught us to ask for it here on earth."

At this point John joined us. "David, I worship this man. He is the Promised One. I feel greatly honored to be with him. But David, being with him is dangerous. He angers our Jewish leadership. He accumulates both followers and enemies in Israel. In gentile territories they fear him but many also believe." The young man smiled but there was a sadness in his eyes. "I can't understand why he antagonizes the leaders but he does it deliberately. It's as if he wants to ridicule the obsessions the Pharisees, Sadducees, scribes, priests and rabbis have with the Law. If that's what he is trying to do, he is succeeding. He has made many leaders very angry."

"Simon … Peter, is this also your impression?" I asked.

"Oh yes—definitely! Jesus seems dedicated to creating enmity between himself and our religious leaders. I think his motive is to show the absurdity of what they have turned the laws into. He especially offends them on the Sabbath."

I replied, "I confess that I quit attending synagogue when I was eighteen. I remember how obsessive our religion is about the law; I have not been an active Jew in a long time. I have felt guilt for that. Are you saying that Jesus himself actually breaks Jewish laws?" I was amazed because I'd seen Jesus and his devotion to prayer. Since he was called Rabbi by some I assumed that he was obedient to the law. However, I had also seen enough of him to realize that he was not "possessed" by the Law as seemed to be the case with so many of the leaders in Jerusalem and Bethlehem. Also, I remembered the profound way he had spoken to me when we met the first time in Nazareth. His purpose was to save the people from themselves rather than from some outside enemy such as the Romans.

Based on what Simon and John were saying he was maybe saving the people *from* the law. What a strange concept! Here is the Messiah saving his people from their own religious leaders! Yes, that could engender enmity with the leadership.

The men went to their homes and the fishermen worked again while Jesus visited with his mother. He would leave and go into the hills frequently. At night I often saw him sitting on the pier. Based on the word of the fishermen, I was sure he was praying. They said he prayed a **lot**. I was thinking, "If Jesus needs to pray a lot—what about me?" So I tried to pray. "Bring your kingdom to earth." I would pray, "Make earth like heaven." The men had taught me the entire prayer he taught them. It was short but called for much. I prayed it with some trepidation, "Give me today the food I need. Forgive me for my wrongs. Do what is your will here on earth … in my life. Help me avoid the tempter and save me from evil." The prayer included humility and praise for the creator. Jesus told the twelve to call God 'Father' as he did. When I asked Jesus about that he assured me that I could think of God as I had my earthly father. That I could call the heavenly father 'Dad' and should feel that kind of intimacy with the God who led the Israelites out of slavery and who was the one and only God. I could call the Almighty One 'Dad.' I found this difficult in my prayers at first but in praying to the Almighty as 'Dad' I began to feel an intimacy that brought peace, comfort and strength.

One day Jesus began to preach from the pier near his house. As the crowds pressed in he retreated to the prow of Peter and Andrew's boat and preached from there. Andrew and Peter had been cleaning their nets while listening to Jesus as he preached. When he had completed his message to the crowds, he asked his two apostles to take him out into the lake and do their fishing. The two fishermen assured the Master that they had fished all night long and caught nothing. I heard Jesus repeat to them that they should move into the lake and drop their nets. But Peter added, "Master, if you tell me to fish, I will fish, but we won't catch anything." I watched from the pier as the men untied their boat and sailed out into the Lake of Galilee. Soon I could see them drop their nets into the water as the Master had told them to do. To my astonishment they almost immediately began pulling up the nets which were tearing with the heavy load of fish. They beckoned their friends James and John with their father Zebedee to come and help. Soon both boats were sinking lower and lower into the water with the weight of the fish. Although I didn't know much about fishing, these men did and they had assured Jesus that today was not a good day for catching fish. The carpenter seemed to know more about their occupation than these four men. Or this was another of his miracles. Then I saw Peter—big, bold, audacious

Peter—fall on his knees before the carpenter. The men got the boats to shore and later told me that what happened was impossible. As men who had spent their lives fishing they assured me that this was another of Jesus' miracles. So here is a man who cannot only heal people from all forms of illness, but who has control over nature and can create fish that were not there. I had not read this in the prophecies. There was still much to learn of this son of God.

25

Another Mission Trip

After spending time in Capernaum during which Peter and Andrew provided Peter's wife and children with food and supplies as did several other apostles, Jesus decided to go out of the city and into the countryside. He allowed his mother to go with them because he was not going beyond her ability to return to her home. As we walked into the hills, we accumulated a crowd. Some of the people had lunch baskets, anticipating the possibility that they might be gone for hours. Eventually we stopped when Jesus found a pleasant grassy hillside and mounted an outcropping of stones from which he began to teach. The people closed in and sat near as they could in an effort to hear the teacher. As time passed they ate their lunches and continued to try to hear Jesus. He was using my favorite teaching technique—he was telling stories. Children were there in large numbers and I think perhaps he wanted them to be a part of the teaching. However, as I had learned before, these stories carried deep meanings that required much afterthought. There were many groups of people and so Jesus would walk from one group to another. He asked the people to sit on the ground in groups and only his followers were to go with him from group to group as he gave intimate talks. Mary and I joined the twelve apostles as we heard his lessons. To one group he spoke of how God blesses those who seem the most unhappy of all mankind: the meek, the poor, those in mourning, the peacemakers, and the persecuted. I listened and found myself remembering the terrible mourning in Bethlehem when Herod had the babies and children killed. It was difficult to see how anything in the form of blessing could come from that mourning. Jesus again left me with much to think about. Because I had followed him from group to group, there were more lessons than I could absorb. I prayed that I could remember most of what he said and perhaps with help from Mary and the apostles we could retain most of his teachings.

Jesus continued to move from group to group—telling parables about treasures and light and about vineyards and women. He responded to questions

98

about the law—explaining that his purpose was to fulfill the law, not to abolish it. The legalists would certainly challenge that! He spoke of the Kingdom of God and about efforts to deceive God.

Eventually people became restless because they were hungry. However, those who had brought food had eaten it and most of the crowd had been there a long time and had nothing to eat. Jesus asked his apostles to find food among the crowd. Andrew came forward leading a little boy who had forgotten to eat his lunch. A snicker went out from those nearby at seeing one quiet apostle leading a little boy forward with his lunch basket. Here sat more than a thousand hungry people and this man brings to Jesus one little basket of food. The boy held out the basket to Jesus and said, "You can have it." Jesus' smile was radiant. I was glad to have been there to see that smile and then see the face of the boy who gave his lunch to Jesus. To everyone's surprise Jesus assigned his apostles to group the people in preparation for a meal. He asked them to find a dozen empty baskets from those who had already eaten their lunches. The twelve came forward with the baskets. They were all empty—I saw it with my own eyes. Jesus looked toward heaven and began to pray. He thanked God for the food and then took the pieces of bread from the boy's basket and began to break them into pieces which he put into the apostles' baskets. Even after all that I had seen and heard I don't think I would have believed this had I not seen it with my own eyes; but as Jesus broke the boy's bread and fishes and put into the other baskets he just kept on doing this. As the apostles began to distribute the food among the groups of people, they just kept giving it out. Thousands of hands reached into the baskets and received bread and fish and yet it originally came from the boy's small lunch basket. The boy's eyes got bigger and bigger. He thought he was giving his own lunch to the teacher and here was his little lunch being served to a huge number of people. I am sure he never forgot when he shared his meal with Jesus. After everyone had eaten Jesus sent word throughout the groups that food should not be wasted and so the extra food was collected into baskets. Those who had shared their empty baskets with the teacher went home with baskets full of food.

In spite of everything that I experienced when I was around Jesus I never ceased to be surprised at what he could do. I also never ceased to be amazed at how frequently he went into seclusion to pray.

As we returned to Capernaum we came to the outskirts of town where the lepers lived in seclusion to prevent the spread of this disease. One of these men came forward, in spite of all laws to the contrary, and approached Jesus. Needless to say he did not have to push his way through the crowds. People stepped aside as the man fulfilled his obligation to shout that he was a leper as he walked forward.

The man knelt before Jesus, who did not retreat upon hearing the word "leper" shouted by the approaching man. His skin was indeed repulsive with the sickness. I stood a safe distance away. The man spoke, "Lord, if you wanted, you could make me clean."

Jesus knelt on one knee and placed his hand under the chin of the sick man. He raised the bowed head and looked into the man's eyes, "I do want that and you are now clean." Although the crowds had shrunk back as the leper approached, they watched intently as the teacher not only failed to retreat at the approach of the leper, but knelt before him and boldly touched the horrible skin. Jesus himself would become outcast for this act because he had become contaminated with the dreaded skin disease. However, when everyone saw that the man's skin became whole and unblemished, it was obvious that Jesus was in no danger of becoming a leper because he had power over the disease.

Word spread quickly through the crowds from those who had seen this miracle to those too far back to see. Jesus found himself mobbed with people wanting to be healed from all sorts of illnesses, real and imagined. He had difficulty even walking. He turned to me and asked me to take his mother home. He then asked his brawny and very bold apostle Peter to help him escape the crowds and retreat to the wilderness where he could have some time for rest and renewal.

Jesus sent the apostles back to Capernaum and went into the wilderness alone. Mary and I both prayed that he would not be gone as long as he had the first time when he returned home almost starved to death. The demands on him were so great and he was growing very weary with so much attention.

While he was gone we began to learn of rumors among the Jewish leadership that Jesus was undermining their authority. Rumors were deliberately spread by these people that Jesus was a fake and that all of his miracles were stories told to the gullible and tricks by his followers. I found myself trying to protect Mary from hearing these lies, although I suppose she learned her share of them at the well. At first I would argue with those who tried to tell me that Jesus was a fake. I told them that I was there and that I had seen these things. All I accomplished was to make those spreading the false rumors include me in the people who were faking all of the powers of Jesus.

26

I Become a Part of the Mission

This time when Jesus returned he had an assignment that included me. He sent seventy two of his followers out to tell about Jesus and what he was teaching. I was sent with another follower named Cleopas, to Bethlehem and several other towns and cities in Judea. I had not known the man before but because he was from Judea we were sent together to our province along with others from both Galilee and Judea.

We left for Judea taking the route I always took—following the shoreline of the Lake of Galilee and then the Jordan River. My first stop was with the group of shepherds I had befriended on my very first trip two years earlier. They had believed my story of the miraculous star and they deserved to have the good news of the Kingdom of God shared with them. I felt inadequate to the task but Jesus had given us pointers on how to teach and I was filled with enthusiasm concerning this gospel of Jesus. I was eager to reach Jericho and tell Bart the good news. Jesus could heal anyone of anything. He could even create food for thousands out of one basket of food and fill nets with fish that were not there before he spoke.

Cleopas and I stopped in Tiberias and had lunch with Josiah and his wife. When I began to tell him about Jesus he stopped me. "David, James and John have told me enough about your Messiah that I am not only a believer but am myself telling others about the Son of God. There is no doubt in my mind that this is the Messiah. Besides, anyone who would choose four fishermen for his team has to be a great leader." Josiah had not lost his sense of humor. But as I thought about it, there was a lot of meat in that statement. So I laughed and added to Josiah's comment that this Jesus had also chosen a shepherd for one of his missionaries. Josiah quickly came back with, "Yes, a worthless shepherd, fishermen, a tax collector, I hear; and now a fishmonger. Your Jesus is my kind of man."

When we reached the area where my friends tended sheep we stopped for the night, hoping to find them in the morning. As it turned out we did not find the shepherds; they found us. The little lamb I had rescued, now grown, was grazing only a few feet from me when I awoke. The shepherds were waiting for Cleopas and me to join them for breakfast. They told me that my little friend had not forgotten me. I rejoiced to be with shepherds and feel the joy of the innocent affection of sheep. I introduced Cleopas to the shepherds and we enjoyed a good meal. We spent the day there with these men. Both of us were telling them about the good news of the Messiah. We shared the wonderful accounts of what Jesus was teaching and the miraculous things he was doing. The shepherds at first said they were only shepherds and no one cared about them. I reminded them that I was a shepherd and yet had even lived in the house with Jesus and his mother. I helped them to realize that Jesus' birth was announced to shepherds and that Jesus was not in tune with our Jewish religious leaders; that he was, in fact, making many enemies among these people. Cleopas and I remained with the shepherds for another night and when we left in the morning there were five new believers in the Messiah and five men learning to pray again after giving up Judaism since their childhood. It was a wonderful opportunity to be a part of this dramatic event in the Jewish world. I felt as if I was a part of a turning point in history; just as the Jewish slaves in Egypt had a great turning point when Moses led them out of slavery and into a new world and back to the God of their forefathers.

After hearing the confessions of these shepherds Cleopas and I baptized them as Jesus had instructed us to do. It pleased me greatly that the first people I baptized were shepherds. We taught them more of Jesus and his wonderful works before resuming our journey.

Cleopas and I departed with enthusiastic vitality for the job Jesus had sent us to do. Our next stop was to be Jericho where I felt tremendous excitement at the prospect of giving Bartimaeus the good news that Jesus could do anything! Anything! After Cleopas and I told citizens of Jericho about the Messiah I would keep my promise and visit the Essenes again before we went to Bethlehem with the message. Cleopas was anxious to go to his home town of Emmaus. Jerusalem would not be in our itinerary. Jesus had told us not to attempt to speak for him in the Holy City. He had explained that he would be coming to Jerusalem and considered the Temple to be one of the highlights of his visit. He added that his mother said she could remember where I lived. So our plans were to cover Jericho, Bethlehem, Bethany and Emmaus. After our ministries in these towns we would return to our homes and wait for Jesus to come. I looked forward to sharing the wonderful news with my friends in Bethany and was especially eager to see Martha again.

As we entered the outskirts of Jericho someone who recognized me gave me the news that Herod had beheaded John the baptizer. The rumor was that his wife's daughter had performed a very seductive dance for Herod Antipas and for her reward she had asked for the head of the prophet to be served to her on a tray during a banquet. Salome was the young dancer's name. She had become sick and fainted when the servants brought in the head of Jesus' cousin as she had requested.

We went to the house of Bartimaeus where we were warmly welcomed. Although Bart was very disappointed that I had come without Jesus, he rejoiced in the message of salvation that I brought to him and believed that Jesus was the Son of God—the Messiah. I was unable to heal Bart though Jesus had told us we had the power to perform miracles. I tried so hard to heal my friend but as I gazed into those cloudy eyes I saw only through my own tears of disappointment at my failure. I promised Bart that Jesus would be coming after us and I knew the Master would be able to heal even a man blind from birth. Cleopas and I told our stories of Jesus in Jericho to all who would listen. We baptized believers in the Jordan. Then we went into the desert to visit the Essenes at Qumran. Bartimaeus accompanied us on this trip.

We were warmly welcomed into the little community of these isolated scholars of the scriptures. Because of all of my studies and the discussions we had held during my period of study there, I was the center of attention for an attentive and rapt audience of these devout people. I explained the many scriptures we had discussed together and how Jesus was the fulfillment of these prophecies. Everything fell into place. The Essenes were overjoyed. We stayed for several days and when we left the group was researching the prophecies for links with our stories of Messiah that these people had spent their lifetimes studying. When we left this assemblage they were in a period of prayer and fasting to celebrate the coming of the prophesied one. And they prayed for us and the work we were continuing. Finally they prayed for Bartimaeus that he might find Jesus and receive his sight.

We spent the night with Bart. Then Cleopas and I wished him health and vision and departed for Bethany.

27

Cleopas and I Preach in Bethany

When we arrived in Bethany we took time to bathe in the creek before I led Cleopas to the home of my friends Martha, Mary and Lazarus. It was late afternoon when we arrived. Normally I would have offered to go to my home in Bethlehem for the night, but our ministry was here in Bethany and we wanted to share our good news without delay. We were welcomed to the home of my friends and invited to share the meal and to be their guests for the night. I waited until we had eaten before beginning my amazing story. Martha was the one I watched the most, but my message was for all three siblings and subsequently for the entire town of Bethany.

"My friends," I began, "you remember during my visits I have discussed the man Jesus of Nazareth. Lazarus, Martha, Mary … Jesus is the Messiah. I have spent time with this man. His birth as a human being and his childhood in Nazareth have been miraculous in such a way as to enable those with open hearts to see that he is the long promised Messiah. I have been given opportunities to see the miraculous works of this man. Now I have been given the assignment to tell others that the Messiah has indeed come and he is none other than Jesus the son of Joseph and Mary of Nazareth and yet the Son of God. Mary, he has performed miracles. Martha, I have seen with my own eyes as he did things no ordinary human could do. Lazarus, I watched fishermen with empty nets that they had just pulled from the lake throw them back into the water at Jesus' command and pull them in so full of fish that it took another boat and its fishermen to pull the in net and gather the fish. I was with Jesus when a leper walked right up to him. He never flinched. He simply touched the man—a *leper*! Jesus *touched* him—and the man was clean. His skin became completely pure. Jesus prays … a *lot*! He says he is talking to his father. Mary, his mother, tells me he is really the Son of God. Angels announced his birth! Not to priests, rabbis, Pharisees. Angels announced his birth to us! … shepherds! God sent gentiles from the East with gifts for his son. Jesus was baptized by John the baptizer before Herod had John killed. I was there and when he was baptized it was like nothing anyone has ever seen before. The sky was dark and overcast. When John spoke the words before baptizing Jesus there was an opening in the clouds and a brilliant beam of light shone through the opening. It fell on one face only: that of Jesus Christ the Messiah. As Jesus arose from the waters of baptism a dove lit on him; and his mother and I, who were together, both heard a voice come from the clouds. The voice was that of God. Of that I am sure. The voice said, 'This is my Beloved Son in whom I am well pleased.' My friends, I am telling you that the Messiah of Isaiah has come and he sent Cleopas and me to several towns to tell the good news. You are my good friends. I wanted to tell you about Jesus as soon as I could. I will be telling all of Bethany about Jesus but I wanted to tell you first."

Mary was the first to speak, "David, you are very sure Jesus is the Messiah. Many of the Psalms sing praise to the one who is to come. Some indicate a 'suffering' Messiah. I've sung some Psalms that seem to refer to the one who will be sent by the Lord for his people. I think you are telling us about this very man."

Lazarus knew his scripture. He cited Isaiah which I had studied thoroughly, "The Lord says 'here is my servant whom I strengthen—the one whom I have chosen and with whom I am pleased. I have filled him with my spirit and he will bring justice to every nation.' This is surely the man you are telling us about. There is a prophecy somewhere that says he would be born in Bethlehem. The prophet Isaiah says, 'he will not shout or raise his voice or make loud speeches in the streets. He will bring lasting justice. He will not lose hope or courage. He will establish justice in the earth.' (Isaiah 42) David, I have waited all of my life for such a man. I believe you have met this man."

Lazarus fed my enthusiasm, "Lazarus, I assure you that this man Jesus is the long awaited one. He is the man that the prophets have been telling about. Jesus himself sent me to Qumran to study the prophecies. The more I studied the more certain I became that the man announced to shepherds and gentile astronomers is the long-awaited one. Mary, Martha, he is coming here. Cleopas and I have been sent along with others to prepare the towns for his arrival. Everything in our Jewish history culminates in this man. Jesus is the Messiah. Herod the Great tried to have him killed as soon as he was born. He spent forty days in the wilderness with God—and with the Tempter. He is here to save the Jewish people. But, as you said, Lazarus, He is here to bring justice to *every* nation." I was talking so fast I was out of breath.

Cleopas, who is a calmer person than I am, spoke quietly, "My friends, the one we have met and are telling you about is the promised Messiah. He does not try to appease our religious leaders. In Nazareth he was well liked until he told the people who had known him his entire life that he was the Messiah. He pointed out their sins. They laughed at him and ran him out of town. He has selected twelve young men. He says he needs them to continue his ministry. He did not ask a single priest, Pharisee, Sadducee, scribe or other religious leader to be one of his twelve followers. He asked fishermen, a tax collector, a shy young man named Thomas. All of his chosen twelve are just ordinary people. And each one, when Jesus asked, simply followed him. Jesus asked others to follow him but they gave excuses and he didn't argue with them but just moved on to another. David and I are asking you to follow him based on what we have told you. We certainly have an advantage over you because we have seen him in action. He heals the sick, casts out demons and some say he can give sight to the blind and hearing to the deaf. We saw him heal a leper. The man's rotten skin became instantly whole at the touch of Jesus' hand."

When Cleopas stopped talking the five of us sat there waiting. No one wanted to be the next to speak. Martha finally spoke, "David, do you know in your heart that this man is the Christ?"

"I know more than I have ever known anything in my life," I replied instantly. "Jesus is here to save mankind. Not just the Jews but all people. He has traveled into gentile territories to share his good news. I have seen him jeered and seen people try to harm him. I have seen children gather around him to hear his stories. I have myself savored every story he ever told in my hearing. When he talks to children he is talking to me. Everything he says has meaning. The more I think about what he has said, the deeper the meanings I see in his teachings. His mother has told me of things that prove he is the Son of God. When she was fifteen years old an angel came to her and told her she would be the mother of God's son. Joseph married her, but God's angel told him that she was already pregnant with God's son. When Jesus was born Mary had never had sex with any man. I was one of six shepherds who saw angels. These angels announced to us—no one but six shepherds—that Jesus was being born in a stable. We went and found him—just as the angels had said. Jesus told me several years ago that his ministry was not what the Jewish leaders were expecting and that when he began his work it would be controversial. He sent me to study the prophets. Everything I learned has been fulfilled just as he said it would. Well, not everything I learned. I hope I don't understand everything because from what I read it seems as if he will be a king without a kingdom. It seems as if he will be rejected. There is much I don't understand—and some that I hope I misunderstand. But one thing is absolutely certain. Jesus is the Messiah. He will save his people—but he has stressed that he is saving his people for his kingdom which he calls the

Kingdom of God. This kingdom does not refer to Rome nor to any known kingdom. But whatever Jesus' kingdom is, I know I want to be a part of it because Jesus is the Savior."

"I believe you. I believe in your Jesus," Martha replied promptly. "And I want to be a part of whatever kingdom he has."

Mary and Lazarus immediately agreed with their sister. "David, if Jesus comes to Bethany we want to meet him. We want to tell him that we too are followers. We will invite our friends and neighbors to come to our courtyard and you can tell them about Jesus and the Kingdom of God."

In spite of the insistence of Lazarus, Cleopas and I went to my home in Bethlehem for the night, having arranged with Lazarus and his sisters to return the next day to talk to a group they would assemble in the afternoon. Uncle Nathan and Aunt Ruth invited us for supper and showered us with attention concerning Jesus. We sat up with them and two of their sons well into the night discussing the Savior and what effects he might have on our lives and on the Jewish people as a whole. It was awkward to discuss this because of the hostility that Cleopas and I had witnessed repeatedly when Jesus was with the Jewish elders and priests. Jesus did not seem to care if he made enemies of these people. He gave them the message and their response to it was not in his hands. As he had pointed out to his followers, the response is never in his hands. Jesus came to save the people but each person makes his or her choice if they want to follow him or not. We promised my uncle and his family that we would try to get Jesus to come to Bethlehem so that they could see him, meet him and hear his message. I wasn't sure if he had time for a small village outside of Jerusalem or not. However, since the angels came to shepherds from Bethlehem, it seemed reasonable that he would detour to my little town—the town of his birth.

The following morning Cleopas and I went to visit other families whom I knew and asked them to invite their neighbors because we had good news for the people of Bethlehem: the infant who was born here more than three decades ago was here to save his people—the Jewish people. Some remembered the slaying of the infants and were disturbed that this person whose birth had caused this tragedy might come to Bethlehem. I reminded them that Herod the Great caused this and that a newborn infant could not be held responsible for events that surrounded his birth. Many of my neighbors accepted Jesus and became followers that morning.

We had lunch with Aunt Ruth and returned to Bethany for the opportunity to tell those gathered at the home of Lazarus about Jesus and his kingdom. I was amazed at the number of people gathering in the courtyard to their home. I had done more of the talking as Cleopas and I went about giving our message of salvation. However, seeing such a large crowd of people I became nervous. Martha saw me wiping my sweating palms on my cloak and came to me with cool water and kind words. "David, don't be afraid to speak to these people. They are our friends and will be your friend when they come to know you."

"Is it that obvious that I am afraid to speak to so large a group?" I asked.

Martha laughed, "David, I'd be willing to bet you are more afraid now than when you faced a lion to protect your sheep."

"Oh!" I stammered, "It shows."

"Yes, it shows, drink this water and I'll introduce you to some of our friends and neighbors. Perhaps it will make you feel better when there are names to go with the faces. Remember, you have a message. Concentrate on Jesus and everything will come out all right."

As she gave me the water she laid her left hand on my left hand and squeezed. Well, I confess that I completely forgot about the crowd of people. However, I almost forgot my message—the woman I found so captivating stood beside me, still holding my hand tightly in hers. I know she saw me blush. I could feel the redness rise to my face. She let go of my hand but gave me the warmest smile I had seen on any woman's face except my mother's. I drank the water and stood on a cairn built for cooking out of doors. The lovely courtyard was surrounded by a wall some five feet high. There was a large tree in its center with Mary's swing hanging from a large limb. The ground was swept clean. Near each corner was an olive tree. On the opposite side of the house was a well-kept garden. With my height and this added elevation, I was easily seen above the group of people assembling in the courtyard. Martha introduced me and asked the group for attention because, as she put it, "This handsome friend of ours has a wonderful message to share with you. This is why we have invited all of you here. David has met the Messiah and his name is Jesus. Jesus was born in Bethlehem a long time ago and his parents stayed with their newborn son at the home of David, son of Joshua and Martha. Some of you may have known Joshua the shepherd and I'm sure many of you wear the clothing created by David's talented mother. She is still known as the finest weaver in this part of Judea. Please give David your attention as he has wonderful news for the Jewish nation."

"My friends," I began. "I am not a priest nor am I a prophet. I am a shepherd who has been given the privilege of knowing the Messiah. When I was eighteen years of age I was in the fields with my father, my uncle and two of his sons along with three hired shepherds. My father and I were talking while the other shepherds and the sheep slept. Perhaps some of you remember the strange star that was in the sky for weeks about a year before Herod died. Dad and I were watching that star when suddenly the sky lit up with brightness greater than full sunlight. We were terrified!"

Am older man in my audience spoke up, "I remember that star and I remember my cousin, who was one of the shepherds with you, telling us about that night. My friends," he now spoke to the assembled group of men and women, "what this man has said is true. That was an amazing night."

When I was sure he was finished I continued, "People of Bethany, the light we saw in the sky was caused by angels. I assure you I am telling the truth. After the event we told people about what we had seen and heard that night. Our friends believed us but we were ridiculed by the rabbi and some of the other religious leaders and we quit telling our story because of the jeering."

The old man spoke again, "All of you know me. I'm telling you: believe this man. What he says is true and I for one am anxious to here more about what that wondrous night means to us now."

This support gave me courage and enthusiasm. "We were told by the angels to go into town and see the newborn baby who was to be the Prince of Peace. We didn't even leave a shepherd to tend the sheep. We all just went to town. Because the angels had said the baby was born in a stable we knew it would be the stable at the inn because there was a census being taken and the town was full of strangers. We went to the stable beside the inn and there, just as the angels had said, lay a newborn baby. Because they were staying in a barn my family invited them to come to our house and spend as much time as they needed with us before returning to Nazareth in Galilee where the father was a carpenter. There is another story that I want to tell. Two astrologists from a country far east of us showed up several days later. They had brought gifts for the child. They had been traveling for weeks because they, like us shepherds, were aware that this infant was someone very special. When these two men came through Jerusalem they had asked Herod where was the child who was to be the King of the Jews. Because they were not from our country they didn't know of Herod's intense jealousy. They could not have known that Herod had already killed some of his own sons and his wife Miriam in order to ensure that no one but him was king of the Jews. When they asked him about the baby he started plotting to kill this infant to ensure that he never became king of the Jews. Some of you still remember when Herod sent soldiers to Bethlehem to kill babies. If you were alive in Bethlehem at the time of the killing of the babies you could never forget it. God protected his son, however, and warned Joseph to take Mary, Jesus' mother, and the baby to Egypt to protect his Messiah. I am here today to tell you that I have spent time with Jesus—the man that baby became—and assure you that he is the long-awaited Messiah. I have seen him heal people. I have seen miraculous events surrounding him and have heard him teach. He is not like the scribes, Pharisees, Sadducees and priests. He is a teacher. His followers often call him rabbi—teacher. He teaches and when he speaks you want to hear every word. He tells wonderful stories. Each time he tells a story I go over the story in my mind again and again because there is so much to be learned from these stories that you try to remember every word he has spoken. He angers the priests and Pharisees. He doesn't hesitate to tell a Sadducee that he is wrong. I saw a leper approach him one day near Capernaum. I was backing away from Jesus because that leper was coming straight towards Jesus and I realized Jesus wasn't going to stop him. Friends, this man's skin looked horrible. It was one of the worst cases of skin disease I've ever seen. Jesus just waited for the man to come up to him. I stayed within earshot but was horrified of being near this man. The man had heard of Jesus' miracles and simply asked Jesus to make him clean." I stopped talking. No one was stirring. I said softly in the silence as these people waited, "Jesus reached out and touched the man. That was it. The man's skin was as clear as mine. Jesus then sent him to the priest to be declared clean according to the law. He was healed the instant Jesus touched him. He was clean. I saw this with my own eyes. Another time I saw him take a small basket of food and feed a multitude of people with it. His disciples went among the hungry crowd with the food Jesus had asked God to bless. A disciple would pass one basket—never refilling it—and yet hundreds of people would reach into that basket and when they brought their hand out it held food. I watched him go to the prophet John who was telling the people that the Messiah was coming. Jesus went to this man and asked to be baptized. What I saw at the baptism was another miracle. The sky was completely covered with dark, ominous clouds. When Jesus rose from the Jordan after John baptized him there came a small opening in the clouds and a brilliant beam of sunlight gleamed through that small opening in the otherwise heavily overcast sky. That beam of light shone on only one person—Jesus. I was watching with Jesus' mother when this happened. She and I both saw a dove come out of the sky and light on Jesus' shoulder. Then we heard a voice that came from the heavens, just as the voices of the angels we shepherds had heard years earlier. I clearly heard this voice say, 'This is my beloved son with whom I am well pleased.' Jesus is the Son of God. His message is to repent and believe in him. He wants us to love one another. He speaks of the law but then reminds his listeners that the law is not an end in itself but rather rules to guide us as we try to follow God. Jesus has angered those who spend their lives doing nothing but studying and interpreting the law. He mocks their obsessions with minutiae of the law because they don't seem to care anything about people but only the rules—their precious *law*. He says that his kingdom is not of this world but I can't tell you much about the kingdom because I don't understand it. I only know that whatever Jesus' kingdom is I want to be a part of it. And I want you to be a part of it."

28

A Surprise Group of Visitors

I suppose I was getting carried away because I was oblivious to the commotion on the street nearby. As the people approaching got nearer to where we were assembled I suddenly realized that I needed to stop talking because this approaching crowd was too loud for me to continue my message. I felt a bit irritated because I was absorbed with what I was saying and I had reached a point of climax. I didn't want it interrupted by a mob of people coming down the street. Because I was tall and standing on the rocks I could see the approaching group earlier than those standing in my audience could. I suddenly recognized a tall brawny man helping push the crowds aside as the slender man behind him approached. Simon! Or I should say Peter—the Rock was leading this mob of people towards where we were assembled. I stood in silence. My audience waited in silence to let this noisy group pass by so that I could continue.

I suddenly shouted, "Master! Master! Please come! I am here, doing what you sent me to do. Jesus, please come and tell these people about your kingdom!"

Peter looked in the direction of my voice and then I heard his booming laugh, "Well, look what we've found here in Bethany! Master, here is our shepherd friend David."

I was speechless. I should have been happy that Jesus had found me and Cleopas here doing what he sent us to do. However, I felt so humbled by the presence of this man whom I revered that I stepped down from my stones. My listeners were now rising from their comfortable places sitting on the grass to see the man I had been telling them about. I wondered if they would feel let down. The quiet man walked to my cairn and stood where I had been standing. Were they expecting flamboyance? Did they think the Messiah would be led by angels? There was no beam of light coming through a hole in the clouds. There was no dove. I felt relief when Jesus began to speak and immediately had the full attention of these people from Bethany who had come to learn about the Messiah and instead were seeing that very man. The people began to sit back on the grass where they had been prior to the interruption.

Jesus began to speak. His voice was strong and clear but he did not shout. It felt as if the entire group had stopped breathing. The silence was profound. Everyone hung on each word spoken by the Rabbi—the Teacher.

"People of Bethany, you today can find salvation. David, my follower and student has been telling you that the Kingdom of God is at hand. The time has come and the Kingdom is yours for the asking. You cannot buy the Kingdom for any price—it is free. But only to those who accept it with all of their hearts. Look at the person sitting beside you; behind you; in front of you. That man, woman, child is your brother or sister. That person deserves the Kingdom of God. Do not store up for yourselves riches on earth, where thieves can break in and steal or where your riches will rot. Rather store up for yourselves treasures in heaven where they cannot be stolen, will not rust and cannot rot. Ask and it shall be given to you, seek and you will find, knock and the door will open." I sat at Jesus' feet watching the people of Bethany as they heard the man I had clumsily told them about. He continued in the manner I was familiar with, telling my friends and others of Bethany about his Kingdom and about the cost of being his follower. I was suddenly aware of Martha sitting beside me watching the Master as he spoke to her friends. Mary had somehow moved so close she could have touched the feet of Jesus. Jesus continued for about an hour before he asked the audience to repent and accept the gift of salvation. As people gathered to tell the Christ they believed in him Martha tugged my sleeve. I eased out of the crowd and into the house with her.

"David, he is wonderful! Thank you for telling us about this man Jesus who is indeed the Son of God." Martha was obviously a believer. But Martha was, as always, practical. "Can you go to the market and purchase food? I will give you money. I would like to have this man Jesus and his disciples as my guests for supper but I don't have food for such a large group."

I tried to stop Martha but she is not a woman easily dissuaded. I agreed to go to the market and use my funds and hers to provide for Jesus and his twelve followers along with, of course, Cleopas, Mary, Lazarus and myself.

When I returned, heavily laden with food, the crowd had dissipated and Mary was in the garden singing to Jesus and his followers. Mary was doing what she did best as Martha prepared to do what she does best. After giving all of my purchases to Martha she ushered me out of the kitchen even as she complained of Mary's uselessness. "But I can help," I insisted.

"This is a woman's job and I'd rather do it than teach a man how to do it. Shoo!" she laughed. So I went into the garden where the group of men seemed to be resting while listening to Mary. Peter slept—snoring loudly. Mary didn't seem to object to his unmusical noise interfering with her lovely voice. In fact, Mary seemed aware only of Jesus, who graciously listened to her Psalms.

Much of the food I had brought required no preparation and Martha's primary task was to cook the meat for the meal. We had figs, olives, bread, sheep cheese, goat cheese, nuts, and lentils cooked with the meat. When Martha was ready she brought the food into the courtyard. Their home was a very nice house but inadequate for feeding eighteen people.

After the group had eaten we all rested, finding any convenient place to lie down and sleep. Very early the following morning Jesus was talking quietly with his twelve young apostles about plans to enter Jerusalem. As much as I enjoyed being with Jesus, I was glad for the chance to spend a little time with Martha. Cleopas reminded me that we still had a mission to Emmaus, his home town, before we had completed our list of towns. So after breakfast we watched the Master with his twelve apostles as they left on the short journey to Jerusalem.

I promised Martha that I would return soon and Cleopas and I made the final leg of our missionary trip as we went to the small village of Emmaus. Here Cleopas did most of the talking because he was sharing the message with his own friends. I enjoyed seeing this quiet man as he led many of his friends to be followers of Jesus. After two days in Emmaus I made my way back to Bethlehem bypassing Jerusalem and Bethany because of my need to rest. I had been on an emotional high for a long time and after my last visit with Martha I was not sleeping well. I lay awake wondering if she would marry me. I needed to go home and rest away from everyone. My curiosity about what Jesus was accomplishing in Jerusalem was not adequate to dissuade me from going home. I knew he would antagonize the priests, Sadducees and Pharisees. Would the High Priest go to hear Jesus? That concerned me.

My return to Bethlehem was not brief, as I had intended. Many of my friends were coming to my home and inviting me to their homes to learn more of the Messiah. The current rabbi surprised me by inquiring about this man I came to represent to my friends and acquaintances of Bethlehem. Rabbi Joel was genuinely interested in Jesus and I tried to tell him some of the prophecies and how Jesus fulfilled these descriptions of the Messiah. Rabbi Joel was young and seemed to have an open mind. I felt relief when I realized I was not instantly hostile to the rabbi. My prayers for a change of heart were being answered. I thanked

God for that and asked him to continue to cleanse my heart of hatred. I stayed in Bethlehem for two weeks.

29

My Marriage Proposal

It had been two weeks since I had promised Martha that I would return. I felt I had completed my work in Bethlehem and so prepared for another long journey back to Galilee. When I reached the home of my friends in Bethany I was surprised to be greeted warmly by Mary. She was filled with excitement about Jesus and was hoping that I could tell her when he was going to return. I had no news of Jesus since she had last seen him and so gave her the disappointing news that I did not even know where Jesus was at this time. She told me that he had stopped again in Bethany on his return trip to Galilee and that Lazarus and Martha had been baptized by Peter along with many other people in Bethany. Mary had asked Jesus to baptize her. Dreamy Mary obviously adored the Master. However Jesus had been gone for over a week and the family only knew that he had promised to return.

I waited in the courtyard for Martha to return from the market. Lazarus was in Jerusalem selling his wares. When Martha entered the gate I rushed over to assist her with her purchases. She smiled more radiantly than she ever had before. "David, knowing you has been a great blessing in our lives. Without you we would have never learned about Jesus. Did Mary tell you that we were all baptized? Did she tell you that Jesus returned and stayed with us again? Thank you David for all that you have meant to our family."

I was elated! Before I could think I blurted out, "Martha, I want to marry you." Well, that was as much a surprise to me as it was to Martha. Mary began laughing. Her lilting laughter was like her singing and both Martha and I joined her.

"David, if you want to spend the rest of your life with a bossy woman, I'm happy to accept your offer."

Mary didn't hesitate, "David, she's right, you know. My sister has always been bossy."

My mind had a flash of the early encounters I'd had with Martha. I then had an image of Mary trying to cook and care for the house without her sister. When I laughed, neither sister realized I was laughing at these images in my mind. "Martha, I will be a good husband and Mary and Lazarus will always be welcome in our home. You have made me ecstatically happy!"

Martha and I set a date for the marriage. With this major change in my life I would probably spend less time traveling and more time at home. For the time being, however, I intended to return to Capernaum and find out if Jesus had other assignments for me in his ministry. Knowing that my wife-to-be was a follower and a friend of Jesus made everything more exciting. I was hoping that Jesus and his apostles, all of which were friends of mine, would be able to attend my wedding.

30

I Return to Capernaum

So I left Bethany to return to Galilee with new excitement in my life. I had somehow proposed to Martha before I had even realized what I was doing. I was eager to share this news with Josiah and Anna in Tiberias. I could hardly wait to tell Jesus and the twelve apostles and especially Mary. Today I would reach Jericho and see my friend Bart and tell him my good news. I also needed to find out if he had found Jesus when he came through Jericho on the way to Jerusalem. I was confident that if Bartimaeus had found Jesus he would finally see his friend from Bethlehem.

It was late when I reached Jericho and I went straight to Bart's house. I called out from the yard to let him know that I was here. The door immediately opened and in the evening light I could see that his eyes were still those of a blind man. "Bart, Jesus was in Bethany and Jerusalem a month ago. Did he come through Jericho?"

My friend answered, his voice trembling with the disappointment, "David, he went through Samaria. He never even came to Jericho. I heard about his stop in Samaria only this week. You were right about his love for *all* people." He said this sardonically. Then the hardness left his voice. "He won followers in Samaria. But if he is willing to go through Samaria then he might never come to Jericho because Samaria is the quicker route between Nazareth and Jerusalem."

"Bart," I replied, "he does not live in Nazareth now. He lives in Capernaum. I am on my way to Capernaum now to see him again. I will talk with him about you because I know he can heal you. I think he would come through Jericho just for you if I asked him. Please don't give up. And ... Bart, I'm engaged."

My blind friend overcame his intense disappointment and his voice sounded even cheerful, "David, this must be the woman in Bethany—Martha. Tell me about it. What does she look like? And David, I will wait for your Messiah to come and heal me. I've been blind for my entire lifetime; a few more weeks or months won't make that much difference. I believe in Jesus. I believe all that you have told me about him. I am now praying regularly—and not just for vision. I am praying for his kingdom to succeed. I know we Jews need this kind of leader."

"Well, Bart, I'll get Jesus here if I have to drag him." I laughed at my ridiculous comment. "If anyone deserves to be healed it is you. I have faith that it will happen." I let that sink in. "Now I will tell you about Martha." I rambled on about Martha's beauty, talents, personality and many other admirable traits until I was sure my audience was quietly laughing at me. We had supper and I went to sleep almost instantly when I lay down. Bart was cooking breakfast when I awoke. My friend accompanied me to the edge of town and was in a good mood as I instinctively waved at the blind eyes still facing me when I continued on my trek.

I did not see the shepherds. This was a disappointment because I was still excited that they had all become followers of Jesus. However, when I reached Tiberias, Josiah's red hair was visible from a distance and I increased my pace to join my cheerful friend.

"David, how are you? I hear you have been spreading the good news of Jesus in Judea. I can see how we Galileeans have a chance at salvation, but I just don't know about you southerners. Could you make any headway with those stubborn and stuffy Judeans?" Josiah never failed to enter conversation with humor.

"Well, Josiah, even though we don't come from Galilee and talk funny like you folks from up north here, we still have a few people with heads on their shoulders and enough humility to admit they are sinners;" I paused, "but only a few, of course. However, I was able to convince the few that I have found the Messiah and his kingdom includes even Judeans. How are you getting along? Is Anna well? And, Josiah, I am going to get married!"

That belly jiggled as I'd never seen it jiggle before. Josiah was laughing so hard he couldn't talk. "David, I don't think you care if I answer your questions about Anna's and my health—not when you end with: 'I am going to get married.' You knew that would leave me speechless."

I laughed, "My friend, I hoped it would, but it didn't work." We spent some time discussing Martha and her brother and sister before Josiah filled me in on the ministry of Jesus and Zebedee's sons. They still joined their father fishing some days and on other days they were with Jesus as he went about the countryside preaching, teaching and healing. Josiah and Anna had been baptized by James right there in front of his fish market. Josiah told me about a woman from Magdala who was well known by the fishermen because she was a very beautiful prostitute. She had seen Jesus and experienced his power to forgive. Her name was Mary. Josiah said she made a complete turn-around in her life and was now one of the women who traveled with Jesus. Her presence offended some people but it also gave hope to many who recognized that they were sinners and realized that Jesus' forgiveness had no limits. I recalled that on more than one visit I'd heard the men in the inn discussing Mary of Magdala. I asked Josiah if this woman was the notorious Mary. Josiah said she was and that there were disappointed visitors who came to Tiberias in search of Mary.

Anna joined us for lunch. Josiah told me that Jesus was spending his nights in Capernaum and so again I parted with my jovial red haired friend. I walked slowly the rest of the trip because I felt meditative. Jesus never stopped surprising me. Having among his followers his beautiful mother Mary, and another beautiful Mary—a former prostitute, was another of these amazing things about the Master. When I arrived in Capernaum Peter was waiting for me at the boat dock. He had seen me as I walked along the shore. When he heard that I was returning he repaired nets while waiting for me.

"David," said the big fisherman, "you have come at a good time. Jesus has been very busy and the work you and we other missionaries did has planted seeds that are beginning to grow. Jesus told a story about planting seeds. He told us that some of our seeds would not reach maturity but if we did our jobs and planted the seeds, caring for the crop and reaping the harvest was up to God. David, the Master is preparing for an important journey. I am glad you arrived before we left."

I had heard enough of Jesus' parables to grasp at least one of the rabbi's lessons from this story. I would give it more thought as I did all of Jesus' parables. I felt some relief that I was not responsible for supervising those with whom I had shared the good news because we had covered many miles. Peter walked with me on to Jesus' home where I found Mary and a beautiful younger woman also being called Mary whom I assumed was the woman from Magdala. Jesus' mother introduced us and I found it hard to believe that this lovely, gracious lady had ever followed her reputed occupation.

In the next several weeks we ministered in Capernaum and in both Jewish and gentile territories in the vicinity. Jesus was beginning to talk of his final trip to Jerusalem. I was curious that he referred to this as a 'final' trip. I was aware that Jesus was extending his mission to gentiles, but he was quite young and I saw no reason for this to be a final journey to Jerusalem. Passover was approaching and we were planning to attend. Apparently a large group of Jesus' followers was planning to attend—traveling with Jesus and his twelve apostles. Among the group were to be several women. One of them, Joanna was the wife of an officer in Herod's court. Zebedee's wife was joining her sons James and John. There was another Mary in the group. She was the mother of another apostle named James. Jesus had encouraged all of his followers who could to accompany him on this trip to Passover. We would certainly be a large entourage.

31

We Leave for Jerusalem

When the big day of departure came, I asked Jesus if he planned to go through Samaria or Jericho. I explained that I had a blind friend in Jericho who had become a believer and was praying for Jesus to heal him. Jesus asked me if I'd tried to heal him and I admitted that looking into those sightless eyes caused me to feel inadequate for such a miracle. Jesus reminded me to work on my own faith. He was smiling gently but I felt shame that I had been inadequate to heal Bartimaeus. Jesus promised to go through Jericho and that he would meet my friend. I was elated! Bart had the faith. The one with weak faith was David. I was sure if Jesus saw Bartimaeus he would heal him.

The journey was slow. We were a large group. Jesus stopped frequently to talk to people along the way and to his own entourage. His message was different. He made references to death. He even stated that he hadn't come to bring peace into the world, but division. His parables seemed to take on a harsh tone. For example he told us that if a tree does not bear fruit it should be cut down and burned. He reminded his followers that the way would not always be easy and sometimes we would be hated for being his followers. As we neared Jericho he wept for Jerusalem, ending with the eerie comment that the proper place to kill a prophet was in Jerusalem. (Luke 13)

I considered breaking away from the group to find Bart but decided that we were probably entering this city with enough fanfare that Bartimaeus, who always knew what was going on, would know well before now that Jesus was coming. I was right. When we approached the area where Bart always walked with me when I was going north I could see him in the middle of the roadway to ensure that no one could get past him unnoticed.

"Jesus, son of David," he cried out repeatedly. "Have mercy on me!" Crowds from Jericho tried to make Bart be quiet. He only called out louder.

Jesus stopped and called for the man to be brought to him. Although I was eager to be the person for this task, I was too far back to get through the crowd to

Bart. Someone brought him right up to Jesus who said, "What do you want me to do for you?"

"Sir," Bart replied, "I want to see."

Jesus' answer was simple: "Then see! Your faith has made you well."

Bart's face suddenly lit into a beautiful smile. I was very grateful that I am tall because I could see my friend. I saw in Bart's face awe and inexpressible joy. I saw adoration. His eyes were clear and shone as he gazed into the eyes of his savior. The mob of people were pushing and jumping trying to see what was happening. I wanted to see the wonder and the immense joy in Bart's face. Knowing the healed man as a close friend put new meaning on this miracle. Anyone in that crowd who had seen the blind man's eyes prior to his healing would know this could not be faked. Bart's eyes were almost white with the blindness. However, in all of the crowding and shoving only those who already knew Bartimaeus or those nearest Jesus when he healed my friend could guarantee that this was the work of God. Bart joined the crowd following Jesus but he was shouting praises and giving thanks to God. I was pushing my way towards Bart when I suddenly realized that I could stand right beside my friend and unless I spoke he would not know me. I smiled at this thought and proceeded to do just that. I managed to get right beside the newly healed man and just watch him and listen to him. He looked at me several times. Finally he said to me, "David?"

At that I just put my hands on his shoulders and pulled him to myself, patting him exuberantly on the back. "How did you know that was me?" I asked. He said that I was the only person around more interested in him than in Jesus. Also I was tall, tanned and grinning from ear to ear. As we continued to push forward to stay with Jesus and his group we saw a man in a tree. He was obviously rich and looked ridiculous on his precarious perch in the tree. Bart told me, "That's Zacchaeus. He's a crook. I've been warned all of my life to avoid Zacchaeus because he'll shortchange you if he can manage it and it is very easy to cheat a blind man."

Well, Jesus again demonstrated that no one is too far gone into sin to be ineligible for his salvation. He walked to the tree and looked up at the man. "Zacchaeus, come out of the tree. I intend to be your guest today." Bart and I didn't know even how he knew the man but were also surprised that he'd invite himself to the home of a known con-artist.

Many people from Jericho began to grumble that Jesus had openly acknowledged a notorious sinner and even planned to eat with him. However, Zacchaeus had climbed that tree for a reason. When Cleopas and I were in Jericho earlier this man had attended our gatherings. I remembered him well because he was unusually short. When he saw Jesus approaching he wanted salvation. His repentance was genuine because he even promised to repay those from whom he had stolen and cheated. How he could keep track of all of them would be difficult, but Jesus announced that he had come to save the lost who repented and that Zacchaeus was saved right then and there. Jesus then went to the man's home.

Bart wanted to wander around Jericho and see all that he had been surrounded by for a lifetime but had never seen. I was very tired. So Cleopas and I went to Bart's home and prepared a meal while Bart enjoyed his new-found vision. From that point on Bart wanted to join the large group following Jesus.

Jesus decided to tarry in Jericho. It was a big city and there were many people to whom he could preach. Cleopas and I had spent several days there but we had only planted the seeds. While he was speaking to groups, a man I recognized as a friend of Martha, Mary and Lazarus made his way through the crowd and interrupted Jesus to tell him that Lazarus was very sick and the family wanted Jesus to come immediately. Peter told me after the man went away what he had said. Jesus told the man that Lazarus was asleep and not to worry.

After spending three more days in Jericho, Jesus announced that it was time to resume the journey towards Jerusalem. By now Passover was only days away and we didn't want to miss that.

32

Jesus Brings Lazarus Back from Death

As we entered the outskirts of Bethany I saw my lovely Martha running towards us. I saw that her eyes were red and tears were streaking down her dusty face as she ran towards us. I tried to push my way forward to my fiancé but was unable to get through the crowd. Jesus spoke to Martha but I was unable to hear what he said. I knew from her expression that Lazarus was not doing well. The group side-tracked into a garden area housing tombs. Jesus asked the crowd to stay a short distance behind him. I then saw that he, too, was crying and knew that our friend was dead. Jesus stood quietly and I knew he was talking with his father. I then saw Martha returning, out of breath, with Mary behind—crying. Mary fell at Jesus' feet. I could not hear the conversation but Jesus took Mary's arm and supported her as they walked into the burial area. Jesus asked loudly enough for all of us close to him to hear, "Will someone roll away the stone from the entrance to Lazarus' grave?"

One of the cemetery attendants told him that it would be very unpleasant to do this because Lazarus was buried four days earlier. Jesus repeated what he had said but this time it was an order. The attendant and several other men rolled away the stone. Most people put their hands to their faces to cover their nostrils. Jesus called, "Lazarus, come out!" I was astonished. I knew the family. There is no way they would have allowed this beloved brother to be buried unless they absolutely *knew* he was dead. Jesus had healed many people, but raising a person from death—after the body has begun to decay—was stretching my faith pretty far.

When the figure emerged from the opening where the rock had been rolled back it was fully wrapped in the bindings used for the dead. I was both awestruck and terrified! The "corpse" reached with its own hands for the cloth that had been wrapped around his head. As he unwound the cloth we saw the face of Lazarus. The young man was smiling at his Savior. Among those present were some Pharisees sent by the High Priest to spy on Jesus. These religious leaders hurried to Jerusalem to meet with Caiaphas, the High Priest. We learned later that there was great fear among the religious elite upon learning that Jesus was coming to Passover. He had a large following with him and he had just "supposedly" raised someone from the dead. Word went out that the resurrected man was a follower of Jesus and surely part of a conspiracy to enable Jesus to take over a Jewish leadership role. The Sanhedrin (the supreme ruling council of the Jews) set up meetings, aware that this troublemaker Jesus was accumulating a following that could cause many problems for the Jewish leadership. There was no question that Jesus was undermining the authority of these influential Jewish groups. If they were to make a move they needed to hurry before Jesus succeeded in again making fools of them.

Jesus and his following could not all stay in Bethany so I invited Jesus' mother Mary and other women to come to Bethlehem and rest in my home. I would stay with my cousin. We would rejoin Jesus and enter Jerusalem with him. Since there was obviously a strong following developing around him, we expected him to use Passover to reach out to a large congregation of Jews with his message about his kingdom.

33

Jesus' Triumphant Entry into Jerusalem

After resting we all gathered in Bethany to go into Jerusalem with Jesus. I found Martha. The two of us would enter Jerusalem together. Handsome young John was caring for Jesus' mother. Big Peter was the spearhead, leading the way and preventing the crowds from pressing too close to his master. Andrew walked with his brother. The various women in the group were accompanied by an apostle or another man because the mob was huge and the women needed a protective escort. Before we left Bethany Jesus sent Thomas and James to obtain the colt of a donkey for him to ride as he entered Jerusalem. I knew this was the symbol of a king coming in peace rather than the militant king who would ride on a horse. This should relieve Roman soldiers when they became aware of the size of Jesus' following. During Passover the Romans always increased the military presence to a powerful force to prevent mob violence.

When Thomas led the little burro up to Jesus some of the women put their shawls over the animal's back. Jesus mounted the animal. It was good that he was slender because the young colt was small. As we moved towards Jerusalem throngs of people gathered along the roadway to welcome the Messiah. They laid their own coats on the roadway and cast palm branches over these and shouted, "Hosanna! Blessed is him who comes in the name of the Lord! Praise the king of Israel!" I was tall enough to see the face of the man wearing the beautiful coat woven by my mother. Jesus did not look like a person at his moment of triumph. His face was filled with an intense sadness. He would smile at the children who ran forward to touch him but it was a sad smile. This didn't surprise me. I had been with Jesus for several stretches of time and could not imagine him comfortable sitting on a throne or wielding the scepter of a king. I did not think I was seeing the kingdom of God because the person who told me about this kingdom did not appear to be at the climax of his career. I looked down at Martha and lifted her to enable her to see the face of the gentle man on the donkey. When I set her back on the ground she turned and buried her face in my robe and wept with me. We did not continue to follow the parade.

We stood together as the noise faded while Jesus and the others walked through the cheering throng of people. Neither Martha nor I wanted to be a part of this event that was filling the face of our savior with such sadness. We turned and walked hand in hand back to Bethany. Neither of us spoke the entire way. Jesus had become so somber of late that I knew he was not the cheerful carpenter I had visited with in Nazareth three years earlier. I assumed he did not like the direction in which things were going. However, having seen him repeatedly demonstrate control over any situation—nature, illness, food supplies and even death, I wondered why he didn't just take control of this situation and show these people what he really wanted. I entered the now empty courtyard of my friends' home and sat with my back against the tree facing Martha who sat in the swing. We still did not speak. After several minutes I broke the silence, "Something is wrong." I said—putting the obvious into words. Again we just sat. Martha offered me food but neither of us was hungry. Still none of the others returned.

It was dark when a small group came back to Bethany. Martha and I had neither eaten nor conversed. We had both been contemplating what was taking place and wondering why Jesus was allowing this turn of events which he did not appear to be controlling. John, Zebedee's son, was escorting Jesus' mother Mary. Lazarus was with them and James, John's brother was guiding the beautiful Mary of Magdala. Lazarus realized Martha and I had left Jerusalem early and so he filled us in on the events of the day.

"Martha, David, Jesus rode that donkey all the way to the Temple. Did you notice his sadness during that event? Judas kept telling the Master, 'We've done it! We've done it!' I knew what Judas meant because I knew that he had been secretly talking with some of the Zealots and was convinced that the following was large enough to overthrow the Romans. Jesus turned those sad eyes on Judas and just shook his head. Judas must have gone back to meet with the Zealots after that because I've not seen him since Jesus gestured "no" to his plans. When the teacher dismounted from the donkey he was at the entrance to the Temple. He went up into the courtyard where men sell animals for sacrifice and he suddenly turned violent."

I was trying to imagine the gentle Jesus as a violent man and could not create a mental picture of that. Lazarus continued, "He went to one of the booths selling calves and to my amazement snatched from the man's hand the ropes used on the animals. He made a whip with these ropes. Martha, he went berserk! He practically ran from booth to booth. He was flipping over the tables the moneychangers were using. Money was flying everywhere. He was freeing animals. He used the whip to chase the merchants out of the Temple courtyard. He was shouting about the abuse of his father's house … and he was crying. When it was all over Jesus dropped his whip and walked sadly from the Temple. I was surprised that the priests didn't try to stop him. Perhaps they were too stunned. Or, if they had seen that mob of people welcoming Jesus into Jerusalem, they could have been afraid of the populace. For whatever reason, only a handful of us followed him. John expected him to go to Gethsemane because he uses it as a retreat for prayer whenever he is in Jerusalem. We went there with him. He made plans to eat the Passover meal with his twelve apostles. Then he asked to be left alone."

I felt a heavy sadness upon hearing this. There had been other occasions in which Jesus had angered the High Priest and his cadre of priests and Pharisees. I knew there had been occasions in which these people wanted Jesus dead. However, only the Romans hold that power and Jesus was not offending the Romans—only the Jews. Martha and Lazarus and I discussed the situation. Mary joined us after a while. She had been crying. Mary had wanted to stay with Jesus when he went away with his disciples. Mary said with disappointment, "He asked all of us to go home. He said he had many things to take care of before Passover. It saddened him that I wanted to stay with him. I was not sure why he was full of sorrow because he certainly had a wonderful welcome when he rode into Jerusalem. However, when he saw what was happening at the Temple he became furious and made the priests very angry." We told her that Lazarus had told us about the Temple. She sat with us as we all sat in silence. Everything was so confusing. I had been surprised at the immense welcome given the Master when he entered Jerusalem. I had not been surprised that he seemed sad about it. Now I was hearing about his anger at the moneychangers in the Temple.

After a while I took my leave and returned to Bethlehem. Tomorrow I would go to Jerusalem and see if I could find my friends and Jesus. John had turned Jesus' mother over to Cleopas who had promised to take her to my home where she and most of the women were staying. I went by the house to see if they had any news I had not learned from Lazarus, but it turned out the women there knew even less than I did. I did not want to upset them by telling them about the Temple insurrection. Jesus' mother probably told the women about that when she arrived later. I saw to their needs and went to my cousin's house for the night.

Jesus had left word with the women not to come to Jerusalem before Friday. Mary, his mother, said he had stressed to her that she was to take Passover in Bethlehem or Bethany. He had planned his Passover meal with his twelve chosen apostles. We agreed to return to Bethany on Thursday and share our unleavened bread and wine of Passover at the home of Martha, Mary and Lazarus.

We arrived as a group in Bethany well before sundown. Martha was preparing the unleavened bread and Lazarus had gone to get enough wine for the gathering. None of us could explain the deep depression that permeated the group as we partook of Passover. I suppose everyone had seen the sadness of Jesus during that magnificent parade into Jerusalem. Lazarus took the role of head of Seder and told the story of the great exodus when God freed Jewish slaves from Egyptian bondage.

34

Roman Soldiers Arrest Jesus

As we were finishing Passover, a new follower of Jesus, a young man named Mark came running to the house. He burst into the silence and reverence of our Passover observance. Before anyone could reprimand the young man for his rude entry he gasped, "They have arrested the Master! The High Priest persuaded the Romans to arrest Jesus. I was nearby, watching when it happened. I knew he would go to Gethsemane with his disciples so I waited there while they had their Passover meal. The High Priest's servant, led by one of Jesus' own apostles, Judas Iscariot, entered Gethsemane. Of course Judas knew exactly where Jesus liked to go to pray." Mark was beginning to get his breath and talked more slowly now, "I was hiding and watching. It was scary because there were armed soldiers and Jewish leaders with Judas. When they reached Jesus he simply walked right up to Judas and said something like, 'Do what you have to do quickly, my friend.' Judas kissed Jesus. The soldiers immediately gathered around him to arrest him. I realized that Judas must have told the soldiers that the man he kissed was the person to be arrested because the soldiers grabbed the Master immediately after the kiss. Peter drew a sword and was ready to fight Roman soldiers to protect the Savior. Jesus reprimanded Peter and made him put away his sword. When they began escorting Jesus away the soldiers looked for the big man with the sword. Peter took off into the darkness of the trees. I ran too because I was afraid they were going to arrest everyone with Jesus." There was a long pause. Not one of us moved or made a noise. Finally Mark continued, "I think Jesus already knew about this. While the disciples were sleeping Jesus was praying. His prayer was the most intense prayer I have ever heard. He was pleading with God to take away this cup from him. As he prayed he was agonizing. I saw his sweat on his brow and it had the appearance of blood. I will never forget his final words, 'Nevertheless, not my will, but your will be done.' I think he knew what was coming"

Mary, Jesus mother, began crying. Martha's sister was wailing. I took Jesus' mother by the hand and led her into the courtyard. "He'll be safe," I assured her.

"There is nothing he cannot do. We have seen and heard of the miracles he has done. He will be safe. I doubt the Romans even have any grounds for his arrest. They were just letting the Jewish leaders manipulate them. They cannot harm him because there is no crime that they can charge him with. The Romans control the Jews—not the other way around. He will be with us for Sabbath."

His mother sobbed into my chest. "He has talked about death several times on this trip to Jerusalem. He never before talked about death—but on this trip he has brought it up repeatedly."

I couldn't think of words of comfort so I stood cradling in my arms the mother of the Prince of Peace and trying to think of words to bring peace to her troubled heart.

Because many of his followers were here in Bethany and everyone in the group anxious about what was happening to Jesus in Jerusalem we determined that we would sleep wherever we could here tonight and the next morning go to Jerusalem and find out what was going on. I was convinced that the Romans would let him go because he had not broken any of their laws.

When morning came our group made the trip into Jerusalem. It was early and the streets were quiet. We found Peter not far from Pilate's palace. The sight of this powerful, confident man dashed any hopes I had worked up. Peter was in the depths of despair such as I have never seen on any man. He looked even sadder that Jesus had on that donkey as he rode into Jerusalem. Jesus' mother was with Mark and Cleopas, Lazarus was caring for his sister Mary and I was with Martha. We went to Peter and asked him what was going on. The man was almost unable to talk. He kept talking about 'three times.' We'd try to get him to fill us in and he'd mumble again about a rooster crowing and 'three times.' I was not sure we were going to learn anything from him but he finally came to his senses and began to relate to us what had happened. We asked him to start at the time of Jesus' arrest. "They couldn't keep him, could they?" I asked. "He has committed no crime. The Romans are harsh but they don't harm people who haven't done anything wrong."

Peter looked at me. "David, I denied him. Three times I denied that I even knew him."

"Peter, what are you talking about? Mark told us that you tried to defend him with your sword."

"He wouldn't let me defend him," sobbed the man. "He—Jesus—wouldn't let me defend him. I didn't know what to do. So I ran. I ran … I ran … away. Then I lied. Then I lied again. Then I lied again and the cock crowed. Then Jesus looked at me. He just looked at me with those sad eyes. And I ran again. And here I am."

We weren't getting a coherent story from Peter but we had learned that the Master was apparently not freed yet. "Peter," said Mark. "What happened after they arrested Jesus? Did you find out what they did with him? You said he looked at you. Where is he now?"

Finally Peter began to give us an account of the arrest and subsequent events. "After he made me put away my sword I got scared. When Jesus let them take him away they were looking for me and I ran. However, I wanted to be sure the Lord was not harmed so I followed from a safe distance. He was taken first to Caiaphas' house. I stayed back to see what happened. Someone there recognized me and said out loud that I was with Jesus. I called her a liar. Later a man said I was one of Jesus' followers. I was really scared because they were still holding Jesus under arrest. So I again said I didn't know Jesus. When it happened a third time I realized that I was probably about to be arrested. The man recognized my Galilean accent and accused me of being a follower." Peter waited a long time. He rubbed his eyes and finally said, "When we were having Seder the Master told Judas he knew he was going to betray him. We didn't understand what Jesus was talking about. And he told me that before the rooster crowed I would deny him three times. I told Jesus I would never deny him. After I ran off in Gethsemane, I followed—at a safe distance. The third time I denied knowing Jesus, I heard the rooster crow. I looked up at Jesus in the balcony of the High Priest's house. He was looking right at me. He was right. He knew I would deny him before we even went to Gethsemane. He knew Judas—the rat—was going to betray him. He knew he would be arrested. I tried to protect him but he wouldn't let me. Then I denied him—three times. He was making no effort to protect himself. The High Priest was ridiculing him and the master said nothing. Caiaphas' cohorts blindfolded Jesus and then would hit him and ask him to prophesy by telling who hit him. Jesus did nothing. After I ran away again I learned they took him to Pilate. Of course there are soldiers everywhere for Passover. Pilate tried to send Jesus back to the Jewish leaders but, because they don't have the power to kill a person, the High Priest is trying to get the Romans to have Jesus killed. The charge is that he calls himself King of the Jews. Caiaphas and those others know that Rome will not tolerate anyone usurping their power so this is a charge that the Romans could actually use for the death sentence."

35

Crucifixion

Peter took our group of about thirty followers including the women to Pilate's palace, because he had heard that was where the Jews took Jesus. We got as close as we could and began asking questions of the crowd milling around. We immediately learned that when Pilate offered to free Jesus as his gesture for Passover the Jews had gathered a mob which had screamed in unison repeatedly, "Crucify him!" Pilate turned him over to his soldiers to do as the crowd demanded. The Roman grounds for crucifying Jesus were that he called himself 'king of the Jews' and there is no king but Caesar.

We tried to find out where Jesus was right now and learned that the crucifixion was to be on Golgotha, a hill near the perimeter of the walled city. Lazarus knew where Golgotha was so he led our entourage towards Golgotha. We were just outside the city walls when we saw the mob ahead of us. There were angry voices and soldiers could be seen among and all around the crowd. We correctly guessed that this was probably the group approaching Golgotha. I was still anticipating Jesus calling for his father to rescue him. I held Martha tightly and managed to push around and through the crowd until we were closer to the three convicted men. We saw them carrying the crossbeams of their crosses. My heart stopped! The man at the front of the procession was wearing my mother's handiwork. I could see him trying to carry that heavy piece of wood. Then I saw blood on the back of the coat. Martha saw it an instant later because I felt her suddenly holding me very tightly and trembling. We followed the caravan but Jesus kept stumbling. Finally an angry soldier turned to a muscular man nearby and said, "Carry that man's beam! We don't have all day!" The man picked up the wooden bar and walked ahead of the procession carrying Jesus' burden with ease. However, the only burden this man had to carry was the cross. Jesus had Judas' betrayal, Peter's denial and the awareness that he was being killed for obeying his father, and not for any crime. After what his mother had told me about his regularly mentioning death, my confidence that he would perform a miracle and escape was fading rapidly. Even with that load being carried by the strong man Jesus was having difficulty walking.

When the soldiers and the three victims reached the hilltop the big man dropped Jesus' crossbeam. There were three tall posts in the ground. The soldiers began by nailing on the top of the center post a sign which read, "This is Jesus—the King of the Jews." Caiaphas' followers told the soldiers they couldn't put that sign over Jesus because it ridiculed them. The soldiers laughed at them and said orders were orders and the sign stayed. When they were ready to nail my Savior to the cross they took off his coat. The usual custom is that the soldiers who perform the crucifixion are allowed to each have a part of the garments of victims. Because Jesus' coat was so well made and was so beautiful they decided to gamble for it rather than tear it up as a rag—or souvenir. I watched three soldiers cast lots for ownership of the most beautiful coat in Israel—woven with my mother's gifted hands and stained with the blood of the Prince of Peace—my master. Then a soldier began to hammer nails into Jesus' hands and I was blinded with tears. Martha had turned her back. Both of us immediately began retreating from the area—but I couldn't get that banging of the hammer out of my head. We were stumbling towards Bethany. I could hear someone screaming in pain but it could have been any of the three being crucified. In my mind that hammer kept banging and banging on those nails.

When we reached Martha's house I did something I never had done before: I started drinking wine and continued until I was drunk. And yet my mind continued to hear it: "Bam! Bam! Bam!" I wondered if I would hear that for the rest of my life. I fell down in the courtyard and mercifully slept. I was awakened by a sudden darkness. Everything suddenly went dark so abruptly that it awakened me. We all talked in the darkness about this phenomenon. I was exhausted and went back to sleep. When I awoke it was light and others had arrived. I realized I was probably not the only one with a hangover that morning. Those who had stayed through the entire crucifixion filled us in on more details. Several of the women had stayed to the end. Jesus had died. Actually they said it was a mercy that he died quickly because the other two were still hanging there and suffering. Then John, who was caring for Jesus' mother, said that Jesus had called out from the cross and asked his father to forgive those who were killing him because they were ignorant of what they were really doing. Because he died before sundown the body could be cared for before the onset of the Sabbath. Otherwise it would have remained there until Sunday dawn when Sabbath ended. Andrew told us that a rich Jew, Joseph, had asked for Jesus' body and buried it in his own tomb. Joseph and Nicodemus were both rich Jewish leaders who secretly followed Jesus.

They prepared the body for proper burial wrapping it in fine linen and putting in herbs and spices that several of the ladies had purchased before sundown. They put Jesus' body into a fine tomb which had never been used. Caiaphas requested Roman soldiers guard the grave so that Jesus' followers would not steal the body and pretend Jesus was alive. We were a very somber group. Now it was Sabbath and we couldn't even go to Jerusalem without breaking Jewish law. So we gathered in small groups in the vicinity of Lazarus' and his sisters' home and discussed what we had learned and tried to make sense of everything that had happened. Lazarus reminded us that Jesus had raised him from death. However, how could Jesus do anything now? He was the one that was dead. I just sat around moping. In addition to everything else I had a hangover. I knew I couldn't drink much wine but had deliberately done so trying unsuccessfully to erase that Bam! Bam! Bam! that continued to ring in my head.

Cleopas was with the group at Lazarus' home. He and I talked about the missionary work we had done. We both wondered if those we had baptized were going to come to us and ask us questions about this person we had told them was preparing a kingdom for us. Martha had begun to try to provide for the group staying around their house. Some had gone into town on Friday and bought food. Martha began to cook and make arrangements for her guests. Cleopas and I discussed our mission trip and wondered where to go from here. I dreaded going to Bethlehem and having those I'd baptized ask me how the Messiah—the Savior—was going to save them when he couldn't even save himself. Cleopas and I discussed that and made the decision that on Sunday we would leave and return to Emmaus. I would watch Cleopas' lead on how he told his converts about a Savior who was now dead.

36

Resurrection

Early on the Sabbath Cleopas and I left for Emmaus. Mary of Magdala, Mary, James' mother and several other women had gone as soon as there was any light to take spices to Jesus' tomb to anoint the body. Cleopas and I were walking alone down the dusty road and discussing Jesus. A man joined us, asking if he could walk with us. We assured him he was welcome. He asked what we were discussing so fervently. Cleopas looked at him in astonishment, "Didn't you just come from Jerusalem? Don't you know what has been happening there?"

The man looked at us curiously. "What has been happening in Jerusalem?" he asked.

I blurted out, "Are you a Jew?" When he assured me he was I began to tell him about the incidents surrounding Jesus. I started with the entry of Jesus into Jerusalem with the mobs shouting hosannas and praises to the Lord, the king and to God. I then told what I knew about the arrest. When I got to the crucifixion the man was looking at me inquiringly. "Surely you knew there was a crucifixion on Friday morning, sir." I said. "I assumed everyone in Jerusalem knew about that. There were two criminals crucified, but the third man was not a criminal. He was the Messiah. I know him and assure you he was the Messiah. We are his followers but now we don't know what to do. His disciples have hidden from the Romans and the Sanhedrin. Cleopas and I are on the way to Emmaus. We came here several months ago and told the people about Jesus—that was his name. We now need to talk with those we baptized because even though I know Jesus was the Messiah, I don't know what to tell these people we baptized now that he is dead." I stopped talking and watched the man's face. There was a flicker of a smile, which offended me.

Then he spoke, "David, have you studied the prophets?" he asked.

"Oh yes, I studied the prophets several years ago because Jesus gave me that as an assignment." I didn't remember telling him my name but I supposed I had.

"David," he spoke my name again, "let me remind you of some of the prophecies. I am not sure you understand all of them."

Again I felt offended. How could this stranger join us, not even knowing what had happened in Jerusalem and then begin to preach to *us* from the prophets.

"Did you study Isaiah?" he asked.

"Of course I studied Isaiah. He was the greatest of the prophets. I spent several days studying Isaiah," I replied.

"Does this sound familiar?" he asked, and continued, "Many people were shocked when they saw him; he was so disfigured that he hardly looked human. But now nations will see and understand something they had never known." I was trying to rethink these words when he resumed, "Who would have believed what we now report? Who could have seen the Lord's hand in this? It was the will of the Lord that his servant grow like a plant taking root in dry ground. He had no dignity or beauty to make us take notice of him. We despised him and rejected him. He endured suffering and pain that should have been *ours*. He was wounded and beaten because of *our* sins. He was tortured because of *our* iniquities. All of *us* are sinners but the Lord laid on *him* the punishment all of *us* deserved. He was treated harshly, but he endured it humbly; he never said a word. Like a lamb about to be slaughtered, he never said a word. He was arrested and sentenced and led off to die. He was put to death for the sins of our people. He was placed in a grave even though he had never committed a crime." (Isaiah 53)

I didn't say a word. This man was quoting scripture that I had studied and I recognized it. He resumed, still speaking words I had studied from Isaiah the prophet: "My devoted servant, with whom I am pleased, will bear the punishment of many and for his sake I will forgive them. He willingly gave his life and shared the fate of evil men. He took the place of many sinners and prayed that they might be forgiven." (Isaiah 53)

He really had me thinking now. Whoever this man was, he sounded as if he did, indeed, know what had happened in Jerusalem. I recalled John's words that Jesus spoke from the cross, "Father, forgive them because they don't know what they are doing." Then I recalled the words that Mary and I had heard come from the heavens, "This is my beloved son with whom I am well pleased". This man had used those same words.

"Did you celebrate Passover?" he asked. When we said we had, he then asked, "Do you understand the meaning of the event?"

I replied that the death angel passed over the houses with the lamb's blood on the lintels and doorposts and these households had no deaths. In houses without the lamb's blood the oldest child died.

"David, that lamb has no blemishes, does it?"

"No," I replied, puzzled at this direction the conversation was taking.

"The blood of that perfect lamb, then, gave life to those who applied it, did it not?"

All I could say was, "Yes, the lamb's blood was the way to life and freedom from slavery."

"When you and your friends had your Passover meal you were celebrating freedom from slavery and from death. Do you believe in everlasting life?"

I felt shame at the thoughts I had entertained about this man. He didn't stop, "Did you study Zechariah?"

I hesitated. I couldn't remember what I had read in Zechariah's short scroll, but I knew I had read that scroll while with the Essenes.

He didn't wait for me to answer. He went on, "Rejoice, rejoice, people of Zion! Shout for joy, you people of Jerusalem! Look, our king is coming to you! He comes triumphant and victorious, but humble and riding on a donkey—on a colt, the foal of a donkey." When he said these words I stopped in my tracks. "Who *is* this man?" I wondered in astonishment.

We were nearing Emmaus. Cleopas invited the man to join us for a meal. This was certainly an exceptional man. I was surprised that I had never seen him among the followers. The man said, "I believe your teacher once told you to take up your cross and follow him." I recalled those words because they had been so harsh. Because the victim carries his own crossbeam, taking up a cross was a direct statement that you will be crucified. This stranger certainly knew Jesus had been crucified. All the words he had spoken proved that. He stated flatly, "How foolish you are, how slow you are to believe everything the prophets said! Was it not necessary for the Messiah to suffer these things and then to enter his glory?"

We entered Cleopas' home and he hurried to get food for our meal. As we sat together the man took the bread, broke it and gave it to us. He bowed his head and prayed, "This is *my* body broken for you." He then poured the wine saying, "This is *my* blood shed for you." When his prayer ended we looked up. There sat Jesus. We had been walking with the risen Lord. I had heard Jesus refer to himself as "the lamb of God." I now understood. Jesus' blood was our salvation from the death angel. He had risen from the grave, even as he had said he would. I, David, a lowly shepherd from Bethlehem, was sitting in the presence of the Lamb of God who takes away the sins of the world. Hallelujah!

978-0-595-47761-6
0-595-47761-5